I0658468

The Rooftop Sutras

Levin A. Diatschenko

**Other books by Levin A. Diatschenko
available from Wolfty & Cliff Publishing:**

The Man Who Never Sleeps

Meta-Detective

Non-fiction articles by Levin can be found at:

www.undergrowth.org

Levin also writes for and edits a free magazine called **'The Veil'**, which focusses on philosophy, metaphysics, the occult, science and historical anecdote.

For more information on works by the author visit the sites below:

www.levindiatschenko.com

www.gamonville.com

Contact email:

aybrus@hotmail.com

where literature and pulp fiction collide

Wolfty & Cliff

ISBN: 978-0-9758071-4-9

Publishers:
Undergrowth Inc & Wolfty & Cliff Publishing
Printed in Melbourne by Flash Print Pty Ltd.
May 2010

Edited by Rak Razam.
Proofed and edited by Dorothy Grimm.
Cover Art and Design by Tim Parish.
Some character names invented by Peter Bagley.

Table of Contents

Indestructible energy

Causality————————————Synchronicity

Space-time continuum

1.

The Playing Card Pyramid

While he was sleeping, Citizen Uccello heard a 'knocking' inside his head. Uccello, like all citizens of his day, only had one dream. It consisted of a single pyramid of playing cards, stacked high and peaceful on a coffee table. But the present knocking shook the image, and the cards collapsed in a heap.

Uccello opened his eyes. After a moment of silence the knocking continued, only this time it came from the front door.

Uccello disentangled himself from his sheets, put some pants on, and opened the door to the intrusive sunlight, which, after a moment receded and introduced the silhouette of a small man. Uccello rubbed his eyes and focused. The silhouette slowly gained details. It was a police officer.

"Morning Uccello," said the officer. His voice was too high and squeaky for that time of the morning.

"So it is," said Uccello.

"You look a little shocked to see a man of the law."

"Are you sure you have the right house?"

"You'd like that, wouldn't you? ... But we've finally got you, Uccello."

"What do you want?"

The officer held up a piece of paper in his chubby hand.

"What is it?" Uccello asked.

"It's a summons."

"A summons? ... I don't understand."

The officer just smiled, faded until he was transparent ... and then disappeared completely.

Uccello closed the door, sat down in the living room and looked at the letter.

Dear Mr Uccello D----,

Re: Revision of Citizenship

We of the courts have recently become aware of your existence. It is immediately apparent that you have evaded all your legal obligations thus far, possibly constituting a serious crime.

You are hereby summonsed to appear before a judge on

this Twenty-Sixth of August, in the year Two Thousand and Seven, for the purpose of justifying your continuing existence. The hearing will be at three o'clock pm, Courtroom Three, the Supreme Court.

If it is found that you cannot provide acceptable justification for the space and resources that you use, or in the case that you do not attend this hearing, your right to exist may be discontinued.

Yours sincerely,

Justice M. Terd

Uccello hung his head and tears welled up in his eyes. When he finally pulled himself together, he stood up and said to himself, "Well, there's only one thing for it … I need a solicitor."

Uccello lived in a rural area. It was so peaceful that not only did the inhabitants dream of undisturbed card-pyramids, but each home actually had a pyramid of undisturbed playing cards on their coffee table. Word has it that generations went by without the cards collapsing.

But on his way out to find a solicitor, Uccello slammed the door and every card-pyramid in the province collapsed. Not realising the harm he caused, Uccello sauntered down the road toward the city, hands shoved deep into his pockets. While he brooded on his troubles, the beautiful sight of the twinkling river and the blossoming trees was lost on him.

The solicitor was a button-eyed man with

a hunchback. To Uccello he looked like a pincushion. His boss must have thought so too, because two or three pins were sticking out of the hump.

"How can I help you?" he asked Uccello.
Uccello gave him the letter. "Can you tell me what this means?"

The solicitor glanced at it and said, "It's quite simple. You're to justify your existence or they'll take away everything that you've been getting for free."

"What does that mean?"

"Have you been paying rent on the space you take up?"

"You mean my house?"

"No – your body. For as long as you've lived, your body has taken up space on the planet, breathed the planet's air and consumed its resources. Did you think that was free?"

"I guess I did. How much money is the rent then?"

"You don't pay in money. You pay in deeds."

"Deeds? What kind of deeds?"

"Anything that might justify your existence. I suggest you get prepared, because the hearing is tomorrow."

"Wait," moaned Uccello. "I'm not sure I've done any deeds. How would I identify them?"

"First you need a purpose. Do you have one?"

"Hmm … no. One needs beliefs to have purpose. I don't have any."

"You must have some."

"None at all."

"Well get some by tomorrow or you can't be helped."

Back at home, Uccello paced up and down his living room. Finally he went to his study and pulled out all his ink and watercolour drawings.

"This should do the trick," he said.

The Supreme Court was a huge concrete cube. It had a single door at the front, which was merely a rectangular hole. Uccello took a deep breath and slipped inside.

He found himself moving through dimly lit corridors, up and down creaky staircases, and passing portraits of judges and solicitors -- pale hunchbacks, their lipless mouths never smiling, their eyes sunken into shadow but the sparks of desire shining from inside them. They looked so thin that the skull was easily decipherable under the skin. Uccello began to worry that he would be late. The signs on the doors were in no discernible order. He'd pass Courtroom Four, then Courtroom One, Courtroom Seven and so on. Some doors were hung crooked or too small to enter.

Uccello finally saw some staff members

wandering around in their black robes.

"Excuse me..." he said, but nobody acknowledged him. Some of the staff passed right through him like ghosts, and others bounced lightly off him like balloons and floated off in the other direction.

Uccello finally came up against a wooden door with a sign that read 'Courtroom Three.'

The room was more like a hall. At the other end of the room Uccello saw a man who was as thin as a stick and wearing a grey wig, sitting behind a desk.

"Come over here!" called the judge, his gruff voice bouncing off the walls.

Uccello closed the door and approached the judge. His face was old and angry and his eyes and cheeks sunken, revealing the shape of his skull.

"Are you Citizen Uccello?" asked the judge.

"Yes."

"Right on time. Very good. Well, don't just stand there boy, have a seat."

Uccello sat on the rickety chair, holding the watercolours on his lap.

"Do you understand the seriousness of this matter?" asked the judge.

"I think so, Your Honour."

"You think so? My boy, do you know what it means to get your existence cancelled?"

"Not exactly. I'll have to leave?"

"You won't have to do anything! We'll do it all for you, me boy!" His voice bounced off the walls and repeated itself – "We'll do it for you!"

"Oh … Do what, exactly, Your Honour?"

"Sentence you to Life in the suburbs!" The judge's shoulder creaked as he raised his hand in a sweeping motion, "Which is to say Death in the suburbs. And the end of you!"

Uccello ran his palm over his closely cropped head, but said nothing.

"You're twenty-seven today. Is that right?"

"That's right," answered Uccello.

"How did you manage to go unnoticed for so long?"

"I don't know. The first time I ever saw a cop was when I got this summons. I always thought they were a fairy story."

"Listen closely. This is your current status." Judge Terd opened the folder on the desk in front of him and ran his bony finger along some facts.

"You have no position," began the judge, "no money, no woman and no prospects. Shall I go on, boy?"

Uccello started to say no, but a wave of emotion took his voice.

Judge Terd's voice bounced around the walls and off Uccello's ears: "Well, boy?"

Uccello cleared his throat and tried again.

"No."

"For goodness sake, boy, you're not going to cry are you?"

"No, Sir ... Your Honour."

"Good. And now, let me get on with it: I hereby charge you with having no good reason to continue existing, for yourself or the community as a whole. Do you understand the charge?"

"Yes."

"Fine. Step Two, then. Can you provide an adequate reason for being granted continuance?"

This was it. Uccello dumped his collection of art on the table.

"What's this?" sneered the judge, and the whole room creaked as he leaned forward in his chair.

"It's art," said Uccello. "Watercolours mostly ... and ink drawings."

The judge took it and perused the pages. "Hmmm," he mumbled. "What about it?"

"I painted them," said Uccello. "But they're not finished yet. If you cancel my citizenship they will never be finished. I understand that the law must regard my work as a potential service to the community. What's more, a potential masterpiece might be among them. Surely, on those grounds, I have the right to go on developing."

Ever so slowly, the corners of the judge's mouth creaked downwards.

"Is that true?" said the judge to himself.

"I'm afraid so," his echo replied, after bouncing off the walls. "The law says that if we discontinue this citizen's existence, the government may be liable for the prevention of a masterpiece. That's murder."

"You are clever, me boy," said the judge to Uccello.

"However," added the echo, "if the art proves to be frivolous, a mere work of entertainment – then it need not be completed; the world has plenty already."

The judge took up the papers again and looked them over. "Hmmm," he sounded. "This has no underlying purpose – just goes well with the curtains."

"That's not fair at all!" cried Uccello.

"Fair? It's splendid," said the judge. "I hereby sentence you to Life in the suburbs, without bail. This sentence takes effect as of right this minute. Have you anything to say?"

"Bollocks."

Judge Terd slammed the desk with his right hand – only, he didn't have a right hand. Poking out of his sleeve was a wooden mallet.

The suburbs were like a vast prison. People were sent there to prevent them from ever breaking the law. Each suburb was like a cell block, the inmates all glossy-eyed and bent over.

On the way there, in the Convict Transport Bus, Uccello asked a fellow inmate, "What the hell happened here?"

They'd been peering out the windows as the bus pushed deeper into Suburbia, now and then dropping a convict off at his or her assigned house.

"Aimlessness, I guess," said the convict, an old timer with a few wisps of grey hair, and neck skin that flapped in the wind. "Sounds a trifle, but boredom spread through the middle classes like a plague. Had very little control of ourselves when these here houses were built, as I recall. Our actions were barely deliberate. The aimlessness made us weak-willed and we went about our existence like an empty raft on an ocean. Pain of the situation made us reluctant to face it, and so it was a relief to let our thoughts get carried away to another place..."

He stared out the window for a while before he continued. "Anyway, because of that, certain repetitions formed. The similarity in architecture throughout western cities, for example; the flow of the population as it rounded its daily routine; the colours and the clothes and the dialogue. Everything seemed like unconscious automatons. More accurately, it was an accidental mass hypnotism."

"And now they're capitalising on it, aren't

they?" sneered Uccello. "Those judges!"

"I used to think that," said the old man. "But not anymore. Reckon they're asleep too. Nobody is in control."

The cell block where Uccello was sent, however, was not much of a prison anymore. The stone houses poked up from the earth in rows upon rows, like tombstones in a vast cemetery.

If you'd ever gone there and wiped the dust from the windows, you would have seen Uccello sitting in his living room like a corpse. He spent his days trying to build a card pyramid, but it always collapsed before he could finish it.

One day, Uccello stepped outside and saw his neighbour rolling around on the lawn. Uccello saw that the man had shackles on his wrists and ankles.

"What are you doing?" he called.

The man shook his shackles off and stood up. He had slicked-back hair and his moustache curled up at the ends.

"Practising," said the man.

Uccello suddenly recognised him: "My God! You're Loudin the Magnificent, the famous escape-artist!"

The man smiled and bowed low. "The very same."

Uccello remembered that twelve months ago a prominent newspaper had challenged Loudin to escape from the suburbs. A huge crowd had watched as he entered the prison/cemetery, waving back and smiling. That was twelve months ago.

"So you're still here, eh?" said Uccello. "I guess not even you can escape from here."

"Nonsense," said Loudin. "I can leave this minute. I stay for dramatic purposes."

"What do you mean?"

"If I were to escape in only one day, the audience would think the feat is easy. If, however, I wait twelve months and return with ruffled clothes and messed-up hair, they will cheer after having figured me for dead."

Loudin picked up his shackles. "Besides, one mustn't try to escape; one must attain and conquer. Would you like a cup of tea?" he asked.

There were photographs of carnival folk all over the walls of Loudin's living room, and a card pyramid on the coffee table.

"How do you intend to escape?" asked Uccello.

"I can't reveal my secrets, but I'll tell you this: The human will can accomplish anything, but only once it gains full control of the mind. Until then there's little hope."

"That doesn't sound like anything I can use."

"On the contrary, that was THE most useful thing I could have shared."

Uccello tapped the wall. "All that's real is what we can touch. Don't talk to me about abstracts."

"If the wall is an illusion then so is your hand. You cannot qualify one illusion with another."

"You're clever," sneered Uccello. "But if you cannot escape from an illusion, it's as good as real. And I still don't believe you can escape."

"Suit yourself," said Loudin disinterestedly. "I bet you believe in the police, don't you?"

"I saw one."

"A product of your mind, a pestering thought-form. Your subconscious sent him after becoming aware of your lack of purpose."

Uccello thought for a moment. "Rubbish. There is no purpose, unless you manufacture a fake one."

"I could say the same about the police."

Prison life was a hellish eternity. Each morning the inmates were herded to the factories and offices where they would do the work assigned to them. Afterwards, they were shuffled back to their cells. One or two days per week they were let out-of-doors where they would pace around and enjoy the open sky. Uccello lived for those days.

The streets were oppressively quiet, and if Uccello ever went strolling after work, the hum of silence made his ears ache. Cops were always following him or watching him from street corners. Whenever Uccello attempted to stack a pack of playing cards into a pyramid, a cop would burst inside the house and knock the cards on the floor. Sometimes, sitting in the silence of his living room, Uccello would hear police sirens passing. The noise would build and build until it was deafening. It sounded as if the police were moving in packs. They yelled out orders and taunts and warnings through their microphones, fired guns in the air and sounded their sirens.

Uccello could do nothing but curl up on his couch and shiver. "We've already ceased to exist," he complained. "What more do they want?"

Uccello visited Loudin ever now and then. He wanted to prod Loudin and find out what he really knew about the nature of things, or whether he was just another prisoner. Besides that, Uccello enjoyed Loudin's company. Morning tea at Loudin's became a regular occurrence.

Loudin didn't say much. He mostly sat on his veranda, drinking tea and watching the street. The silence was unusually rejuvenating; the police never seemed to show up there.

"You don't talk much," Uccello said one day, breaking the mood.

"No," said Loudin.

When no explanation came, Uccello asked:

"Well? Why don't you tell me about your escape method?"

"There's no point. You will believe nothing you haven't experienced yourself."

"If you tell me your method, I can then try it out!"

"The only useful kind of talk is debriefing— and you haven't done anything to debrief. Try to escape yourself, and then if it fails I will talk."

"And if my method doesn't fail?"

"Then you won't need to talk."

The next day, Uccello went to visit Loudin again, but he did not answer the door. Uccello knocked harder and the door creaked open. The house was empty. Left behind were a few carnival photographs and the card pyramid still intact.

After gazing a while at the pyramid, Uccello returned to his cell.

The routine ground away at Uccello. He decided to escape before he was reduced to dust.

Using the money he had saved from working, Uccello bought himself a rusty old car that would be entirely adequate for the one-way trip. He filled it with food and hit the road.

As Uccello came to the edge of the suburbs, a sign reared up from the bitumen: "You Are Now Leaving Suburbia".

Uccello swerved and missed it by an atom or two.

Uccello had not zoomed one hundred kilometres down the highway before he saw the smoke cloud of a band of police cars in his rear-view mirror.

The sirens began screaming.

Uccello stepped on it and tried to lose them. But the farther he got, the longer the line of cops pursuing him became. "By the amount of cops I attract you'd think I did exist, and that I was important."

It was no use. The police were catching up. The sirens screeched loudly, and Uccello felt fatigued. He turned the car radio on and up, in order to drown the sirens out.

The entire hoard of police cars vanished without a trace.

Nothing could be heard except Uccello's car radio. Uccello pulled over. He got out of the car, peered up the road, and found that he was still alone.

"I can't believe it!" he exclaimed. There wasn't a trace of the police. "What happened?"

Without the slightest spark of understanding, Uccello hopped back into his car and continued on his road to freedom. He turned the music up and bopped his head.

Later that night, Uccello parked away from the road and slept. When sunlight hit him the next morning, he opened his eyes.

Looking around, he had an uneasy feeling. He left his car where it was and walked out to the road to take a look.

He heard engines revving. Then he saw a dust cloud. Within seconds the cloud grew larger and carried with it a pack of snarling police cars.

Uccello bolted back to the car. Sitting in the driver's seat, he listened and waited … hopefully the cops would pass him by.

Sirens sounded. More police cars burst into view and screeched to a halt around Uccello's car – he was surrounded in seconds. Looking right into the eyes of his captors, Uccello saw that they were shaking with laughter.

Uccello fumbled for his key and turned the engine on. He would still go through the formality of resisting till the end.

The night before, Uccello had not turned the radio off. It simply went off with the car engine. Therefore, now – when he jerked the engine back on – an early morning talk show that was on the radio also came on. " … Marvellous day ahead of us," the host was saying, "Absolutely brilliant …"

Uccello found himself alone again. Even the dust from the police cars seemed to have vanished.

"Where the fuck did they go?" he gasped.

"We'll be playing the same classic rock songs

again and again and again … all morning long!"
said the radio.

Uccello revved the car, steered it back to the
empty highway and drove it to the horizon.

After a night and a morning of straight driving,
Uccello arrived at the outskirts of a new town. He
saw cattle and fences, signs and a few shacks. On
the horizon he saw rooftops.

Without warning, a street sign reared up at the
car. It said, "Welcome to Suburbia".

Uccello swerved and went white. He recognised
the streets. But how could that be?   Street by
street, Uccello felt sicker and sicker. This place
was exactly the same as the town/prison he'd fled
from, right down to every loose brick.

When Uccello arrived at his own house, he
opened the car door and vomited into the gutter.
He saw that his hands were shaking.

As he dragged his feet toward his house, he
saw a police car parked across the road.   When
he opened the front door, entered and closed it
behind him, he heard the cops drive away.

Uccello looked around him. It was his home
all right.

"It doesn't make sense. How'd I end up here?"
he asked himself. "It was one road without any
turns!"

He went to bed, assuming his death pose.

Later that day, Uccello climbed onto the roof and dived off. Perhaps it's the only way out, he mused.

He seemed to sail down peacefully, accompanied only by the hollow sound of the wind. It felt good, but with a pinch of fear.

He slammed into the ground. Everything went black.

Within the blackness, gradually a pinpoint of light appeared. It grew larger and larger, until Uccello felt that the darkness was a tunnel, leading towards the light. It was an opening.

Uccello zoomed into the opening of light. It was so bright that all he could discern was whiteness. He waited and floated in the whiteness. Finally the harshness of the light lessened and Uccello began to see forms. He felt that he was standing on solid ground again. The light retreated into a sphere that hovered high in the distance … surrounded by a blue sky. A sun.

Uccello then looked down from the sun… And he saw his house.

"Fuck!"

Uccello was 'alive' and standing in the street. He fell to his knees and sobbed.

He seemed to have 'reincarnated' into exactly the same situation he had known before. So much for escaping, he thought.

He awoke at noon the next day and read the newspaper. There was an article about Loudin the Magnificent's "Brilliant escape from the suburbs".

"Smug bastard," said Uccello. "Wonder how he did it."

Uccello then looked at his scattered deck of cards. He knew he should make the attempt to build a pyramid, but for now he just didn't feel like it. So he put on a shirt and went for a stroll outside.

The suburb was stagnant. Uccello kind of liked that; it reflected how he felt. He strolled around the block peering inside various houses; he saw many tables with cards scattered over them. Sometimes there were half-built pyramids. The Suburbanites had their radios and televisions on constantly. Drivers had their car radios on too.

One needs Background Noise to get by in the suburbs, he thought. Police seemed to avoid the 'choppy waters' of tumultuous soundwaves, but they swarmed to any gap of silence.

It occurred to Uccello that Loudin was the only person he met in the suburbs who had successfully built and maintained a card pyramid. Moreover, Loudin was neither bothered by police, nor was he a user of Background Noise.

Uccello remembered Loudin's remark. He went

back home and looked at his scattered cards. How can I do things like escape when I cannot even rebuild my cards?, he thought. And how can I rebuild my cards if I cannot even maintain the pyramid in my mind?

First I must attain the representation of the pyramid in my mind, then I must conquer the cards in my living room. Attain a pyramid of the ones in my living room then conquer the prison and the police. Attain and conquer, attain and conquer, again and again...

So, each night and each morning, Uccello sat in a chair and closed his eyes. He visualised a deck of playing cards and, one at a time, he pictured himself building them into a pyramid.

The distant sounds of the police interrupted him countless times, but the more Uccello practiced, the stronger his willpower became – and thus the stronger his concentration became.

Eventually, he built a full pyramid inside his mind.

It became stronger by degrees until Uccello visualised snowstorms and hurricanes attacking the pyramid with no effect. The pyramid held sturdy!

During his days off work and in the evenings, Uccello sat at his coffee table and carefully worked on his actual card pyramid. Ever so slowly the first floor was attained, and the next started on. But he knew the whole deck of cards would take months to finish, so Uccello just balanced a card or two (maybe four on a good day) per sitting.

During this 'constructive' period, while out walking, Uccello came upon an old friend and fellow artist. They clung to each other and wept.

"What are the chances!" Uccello said, "that we would be sentenced to the same suburb!"

Hanna had been an artistic activist. After the bout of depression following her arrest (she was arrested two years before Uccello), she resumed her activism in Suburbia. Her plans involved breaking into establishments and homes and leaving card pyramids there to be discovered in the morning. She attempted to leave pyramids in the middle of traffic intersections, and to climb onto houses and drop cards over the streets. Uccello told Hanna of his escape attempts and his current card-stacking discipline.

They met every now and then for coffee, in cafes where the music was always on and the volume always turned up. He looked forward to their get-togethers. She seemed to, as well, always rambling enthusiastically about her latest venture. She couldn't understand why Uccello didn't participate.

"That's all very well, you building that

pyramid," said Hanna, "but what about the rest of the suburb? It's not going to beat the police force."

Uccello did not defend himself. He didn't feel he needed to; she wasn't judging him, she was inviting him.

Hanna went on to explain that card pyramids were impractical, anyway. "All the pyramids I've tried to build in houses or in public places blow down or collapse before I'm even finished," she said.

"That's the point," said Uccello.

"So, I've moved on to radios. I break into buildings and plant blaring radios in the middle of the floor and the cops are blasted clear. You should see it!"

On some days, Uccello would see Hanna's accomplices walking around with ghetto blasters in a show of rivalry to the police gangs. In their wake, police seemed to gather like darkness around a dying flame.

"I admire what you're doing," said Uccello to Hanna on one of their get-togethers, "but don't you ever crave silence?"

"There is no silence, silly!" she said. "Do you want to attract the cops? The choice is either noise or cops."

Then he told her about Loudin the Magnificent,

and how his home had neither of the choices.

"Wow! You actually met him out here?" Hanna's eyes lit up. "He must have had some background noise, surely?"

"I can't recall any. His home was so peaceful …"

Later that night, Uccello came home to discover his house had been broken into. Debussy's opera 'Pelléas et Mélisande' was playing through the house. Uccello didn't mind that at all.

Hanna was waiting in his bed with a smile on her face.

Hanna stayed with Uccello often after that. She watched him in the mornings while he carefully placed cards on top of cards, picked up the ones that had fallen and tirelessly rebuilt them.

Uccello came to realise that when Hanna was around, there were fewer cops about the place, and when she was gone there were twice as many as before. He hated being without her.

"It's true," he confessed one night. "Though I don't believe in your methods, it's as if your presence alone is a force that cannot be imprisoned for long."

Shocked, she said that she thought the same about him. "It's not me who the police are avoiding!" she said. "It's you! I've never been so at peace than when I'm lying here with you."

"Maybe we ought to build a collective card-pyramid," mused Uccello.

"Wow, that's it!" said Hanna. "We could see our culture and civilization as a cooperative art form, you know, that you would refer to in the same way as, say, Egyptian Art or Mayan Art. You follow? This way the suburbs would cease to exist."

"I'm following," said Uccello.

More and more, Uccello worked on his deck of cards. It got to the point where he'd be up most of the night working on them. In the beginning they had collapsed every time he'd gotten to the third level. But now, he was reaching the fourth and even fifth levels before his attention and hands started shaking. When that happened, he'd leave it alone for the night – if he were patient, that is. If he weren't, he'd continue and end up knocking the whole thing over again. It was all about patience.

Hanna came into the living room one night and said,

"Aren't you coming to bed?"

Uccello looked up with bloodshot eyes. "Oh," he exclaimed, "what a wonderful thing is perspective!"

Uccello's coffee table pyramid was almost complete. The structure only needed three more cards on top. They would form the triangle at the peek, but the interruption had shaken Uccello's concentration … and, just to be safe, he left the three cards alone, to be finished tomorrow.

Hanna and Uccello hadn't seen a police officer in months even though they'd ceased using Background Noise. They were living in a calm bubble of silence.

"Perhaps its time for us to disappear," said Uccello.

"There's nothing to stop us," said Hanna. "The police seem to have disbanded."

When Citizen Uccello finally disappeared from Suburbia, he left behind an indestructible card pyramid on his coffee table. Next door, Loudin's pyramid is also still standing. Across the suburbs more and more houses attained card pyramids and the peaceful aura of strength that came with them, until eventually each house had one.

In time, the streets and houses became more like an art gallery than a prison. Each street, public place and private home, was decorated with card sculptures.

People still visit the empty suburbs to gaze at the beauty there – and to wonder what kind of people once inhabited them. They are no less mysterious and awe-inspiring than the ancient Egyptians or the Mayans. Why did they vanish? Where did they go? Perhaps we'll never know. Perhaps we will.

2.

The Initiation

A town like any other. The turn of the century. The same thing each day.

Every house on the street was more or less identical and lately I'd been having trouble finding my way home. My younger brother had a white ute, so I'd search for the driveway with my brother's car in it. There was more than one white ute on the street but my brother's had a dent in it, near the fuel cap, and I always remembered the shape of the dent. When my brother took his ute out, I'd pick a house at random.

I'd recently opened my mind to the concept that time may in fact be simultaneous: all things are happening at once, all times exist together simultaneously. This disturbed me because if it were simultaneous, that would mean that the past does not fade out of existence behind you; it exists forever in its place. So in one sense I will live there for eternity. In the past I still do, if you follow.

So I began a strict routine of strolling around the block every evening in order to practice paying attention to where I was in the present. If I could achieve that old trick, I would be able to stop myself from suffering an eternity. I tread along slowly with my hands clasped behind my back, and my feet in comfy kung fu slippers. I paid attention to aromas of trees and flowers, and the cooking from the houses I passed. I looked at the stars, felt the breeze. I memorised house numbers and sometimes even counted my steps. It wasn't easy. The mind is like a disobedient dog and I constantly drifted into daydreams – specifically either nostalgia for the past or fantasies of the future.

People are always saying to live in the present. It has become a catchphrase. But it's not till you earnestly attempt to do so that you learn that it cannot actually be done without the dedication of an athlete. Being a yogi is not holding a certain opinion about the world, it's being an athlete of the mind.

The more I did stay present the more I began to feel the presence of a hidden power encouraging me not to. An adversary. Incidents would even pop up just before I was to set out on my walk. The telephone would ring to delay my leaving. A television show that I'd been meaning to catch would 'conveniently' come on.

One night it was particularly bad. I'd gotten halfway through my walk and I could barely remember getting there – such was my lack of concentration. I snapped back to attention upon hearing a violent exchange between two long-grassers. Because I was poised for the possibility of trouble, I maintained attention. One was a man and the other a woman – presumably his wife. Both were haggard. They stood spewing froth and bad language into each other's face. Within a minute of starting, the argument switched, almost naturally, into a fistfight.

There was a clinch and both came toppling down. I passed by as they lay on the road, the woman on the bottom, blaming each other for what just happened.

Later, when I was well past them, I drifted again into a stream of thought. Then a car sped by and threw mud up at me – snapping me out of it. For another minute or so I grumbled in the discomfort of my wet pants, but soon enough I drifted off again...

This time a loud crash brought me back. Just up the road were two cars facing each other, panels bent, headlights shattered and broken glass sprinkled all over the scene.

"For fuck sake!"

"You bloody idiot!"

I watched as the drivers inspected each other's vehicle – a sports car and an upmarket van. The drivers exchanged insults, and then numbers on paper. They then drove away … and, likewise, off went my mind again....

Next, the very house I was in front of came alive with the sounds of shouting within. It was an elevated pre-Cyclone Tracy house. I could hear things being smashed and apeals from what must have been a football fan watching the television.

It was now that I began to suspect something else was going on – and sure enough the house quietened down again. There was a second power at work, doing everything it could to keep me from daydreaming. An ally. While I was paying attention, the streets were morbidly quiet; but as soon as I drifted something happened to jolt me back.

From then on, my suspicion kept me in the present moment. A few thoughts and images popped into my mind but I quickly banished them.

For awhile there was only silence, and then I

heard a telephone ringing.

I ignored it and continued walking, counting my steps to keep concentration. The ringing came from behind but did not fade as I made ground. Finally I turned and saw that it was, in fact, my own telephone – sitting there in the middle of the road; it had followed me all the way from home. The chord trailed down the street leading back home.

It rang louder. It had always been demanding but this time it was scary. I knew this had to be the work of the first power, and my heart doubled its speed. They couldn't get me dreaming anymore so they were trying something else. I was onto something big. I approached the phone and picked the receiver up.

"...Hello?"

"Hi there, Louie. This is Dave."

Dave was my boss. "Hello Dave..."

"I need you to come in to work."

"I already did morning shift."

"Come on, Louie. You want more hours don't you?"

"I..."

"Sure you do. More hours is more money. What are you going to do with all that spare time? Besides, we really need you, buddy. I'll expect you in half an hour?"

I was about to give in and say yes when a car

screeched around a corner, and my eyes glanced straight up at the licence plate, which said simply: "Escape".

I slammed the phone down, turned and ran. The phone rang behind me but I refused to look back.

My shirt was soaked in sweat now, and the ringing was so far away that it faded completely. But then I heard the public telephone in front of me ring.

Fuck this, I thought. I'm in some kind of serious shit.

I stopped and took a deep breath, then looked around. This was ridiculous. I went in, picked up the receiver and put it straight back down again. That'll fix 'em, I thought.

This was all very tiring on my nerves, so as I went on I was delightfully surprised that the streets returned to silence.

When I rounded a corner to my own street, there was my telephone again – sitting on the driveway of one of the yards, waiting for me. It wasn't ringing, though. As I moved closer, it backed away and hopped back towards the house.

Wait a minute, I thought. Is that my house?

Yes, there was that pot plant that I had recently moved from one windowsill to another. But my front door was open – and I didn't remember doing that.

I walked inside to see a stranger sitting on the couch. The telephone was back in place.

"Mr. Trad?" said the stranger. He was chubby and wore a dark suit and sunglasses. I didn't know anyone who wore a suit. Judging by his greying hair, I'd say he was approaching middle age.

"What the bloody hell are you doing in my home!" I barked.

He stood up and flashed me a badge, said his name was Detective Such-and-such.

"What's going on?" I asked.

"I'm sure it's nothing serious," he said in a high and squeaky voice. "We're just a little concerned, so I've come for a chat."

"What are you talking about? Has something happened?" I was worried about my mother and younger brother.

"Have a seat," said the cop. I shouldn't have, but I did. He remained standing as he continued: "There's been reports, Mr. Trad, that a pot plant at this address has been moved."

This took me by surprise, but I finally responded: "Yes. Why, I moved one the other day – the Devil's Ivy. But I don't understand..."

The cop leant over me and took his sunglasses off. His eyes were grey and, shall we say, deliberately unfriendly. "There's nothing to understand," he said slowly and clearly. "I'm just letting you know that we noticed the change ... and that we liked it better where it was."

"What are you talking ... are you serious?"

He put his glasses back on and went to my television. "I'm just letting you know, that's all, Mr. Trad. If you understand that then there won't be any need for further action."

With that he switched the television on, turned the volume up and walked straight out the front door. I stood at the window and watched him walk to the street. A car rolled up, he jumped in, and then it sped away.

My mother and younger brother came home soon after to see the wreck of me sprawled over the couch. My mother, squinting into her glasses, immediately turned the television down. "What are you doing with the volume so loud?" she said in her South American accent. "Are you stupid or something?"

My brother started opening windows. "You got something against fresh air?" he asked.

My mother tinkered around in the kitchen and my brother wrestled off his steel-capped work boots. They then seated themselves around me. Gossip began about work and our lives. Soon the television joined in the conversation and I could no longer tell who was saying what.

I had to get out.

"Where are you going?" a voice called.

"Nowhere," I replied. "Just to the yard."

It was dark by now. I can't remember the reason, but for the first time since I left school I looked up and saw the sky.

"Holy shit!" I yelled. It seemed so much bigger than it did on television. The stars were out in truckloads.

The sky made me feel trapped in some pit or trench. My line of vision led me to the roof of the house and I concluded that I should climb onto the roof to get out of the pit.

"Louie! Phone call for you!" my brother called.

Yeah, I thought. I bet there is. "Tell them I'm out!"

I went back inside, grabbed the keys to my brother's car (the white ute) and then parked it close under the eve of the roof, against the house. Then I used the car to climb onto the roof of the house.

It was like lifting myself out of a fog. My heart was aflame. But it was thrown by disorientation: I wasn't sure where I was. This did not vanish until I looked down and received some understanding through the bird's-eye view. I had, in fact, climbed out of my life, which comprised of only a small number of pastimes, streets and buildings; a small and familiar track I would round everyday, slightly altered on weekends. I never climbed onto roofs.

I suddenly felt as if I had no identity and I found myself asking: "Who am I?"

Looking down from the roof, I could see a long queue of Louie Trads, each from a slightly different time frame – like the still drawings that make up a moving cartoon. When I focused on all the Louies as a whole, it resembled a stream. A blue stream, mostly, because of the blue overalls I wore each day to work. The stream began at home, ran around my series of streets and buildings, looped itself and then returned.

I panned my vision across the town and saw a vast area where the blue stream of Louie Trad never flowed. That's no good, I thought.

Then I looked at the other streams with their respective colours. They ran on slightly different routes than my stream, but they all kept to the same overall area – close to the main roads and biggest buildings. Together the streams formed a river with a well-established riverbed.

"That's no good at all," I announced, deciding to address the town.

To my surprise, the town replied.

"…I'm tired," sounded a voice in surround sound.

"Who said that?" I demanded.

"Me," the voice replied. "The city. And boy… (yawn)…am I pooped." The voice rose like steam from the anonymous streets.

"You're the city?" I asked incredulously.

"That's right. I'm… boy, I'm tired…"

That's about all it said. I tried quizzing the town and finding out more – its plans and philosophies – but it wasn't interested in questions, it was just glad to have an ear to unload its troubles on.

Ignoring the voice, I decided to have a good old look at the rest of the streets – the areas that lay outside of the human 'river'. And as if I wasn't depressed enough, I discovered the dams. Basically there were tall, brick dams running parallel to the "river", holding the river on its automatic course. Thinking back through the years I've lived here, I can't remember ever being aware of these dams. Only now that I was out of the time stream did I notice it.

"Fuck this!" I exclaimed.

"Sooooo tiiirrrrreeed," the city moaned in reply.

I felt like reaching down and pulling everyone onto the rooftops. All those choked lives running breakneck on the aimless current. I read somewhere that when the Saviour comes everyone will dance on the rooftops. But it's got to start with someone, so I jumped to my feet and moshed to my own singing. I sang the "Ode To

Joy" part from Beethoven's Ninth. But nothing changed.

When I finally jumped down from the roof and back into the identity of Louie Trad, daily life resumed as normal. I still had trouble finding my home at the end of the day, and I still went for my evening strolls. Apart from the telephone occasionally following me down the driveway, nothing out of the ordinary happened.

One night, after the late shift at work, I was driving my brother's ute. I suspected the car behind was tailing me. An arm reached out and put a siren on the roof. It flashed red as the car sped up beside me: the same cop that had come to my house.

"Pull over," he squeaked, and I obliged.

We stood outside our vehicles, me in my filthy overalls and him with the same dark sunglasses on, even though it was night. I leaned against the ute, arms folded against my chest.

"What's the problem?" I asked. "Another pot plant?"

"Listen son," he started. His head was low and his hands were shoved into his pockets. He looked like a father reluctantly setting his son straight because of the iron wife. "You are what we on the Force call a slow learner. You understand what I'm saying?"

"Not really."

"Well now," he said hitching his belt. "I don't think I have your full attention yet." He came up to the ute and without a moment's hesitation kicked his heel into the side.

"Shit!" I yelled. "Alright! You have my attention!"

"Now what the hell is that stink?"

"That's probably me. I just got off work."

He took a couple of steps back.

"Anyway," he resumed. "I'd better get right to the point. Have you by any chance been jumping around on roofs lately?"

I felt a sudden jolt of nervousness. "Um...no. Well I was on the roof of my house the other day, but there was no jumping involved. And it was only my own roof, no one else's."

"Let's see," he said and took a step towards me, but then he remembered my stench and stayed put. "I'm guessing that you saw the river?"

"No. Not really. I might have – if we're talking about the same thing."

"Uh-huh. Yep. Listen, Mr. Trad. I'll tell you what I'm going to do. I'll spell it all out to you just so you understand, because I don't think you really mean any harm at all. Okay?"

"Okay." It's best to comply in these situations.

"Alright." He paused and raised his index finger. He began slowly but picked up momentum as he went along: "People do not climb on roofs except to fix them. People don't lie on floors – only dogs do that. People don't walk long distances. People never try their voices at top volume … except of course during sanctioned activities such as professional singing. …People likewise do not push their muscles to full capacity. People, uh, do not stop eating for any longer than the breaks between the three square meals of the day; nor do they go more than eight hours, tops, without speaking; the same with washing; the same with television. Now let's see … ah yes. People answer their telephones. Are you with me?"

"Yes sir," I said.

"People do not engage in any activity without a logical reason for doing so. Now, you remember those dams, son?"

"Yes. Keeping the river on course."

"No. There aren't any dams – those are just billboards. They only look like dams from outside the time stream. Are you with me?"

"With all due respect, I know what I saw. What about free speech?"

"Free speech within safe borders is fine. People, Mr. Trad, do not discuss anything outside of the river – and people don't leave the river. If they are restless – the river runs all over the world. You can always move from one vein to another. Backpackers do it all the time. Just don't leave it.

And most importantly of all, Mr. Trad: People do not under any circumstances leave their identities. I cannot stress this enough. Okay – Mister Trad?" He emphasised my name, as if to rub in the fact that it was my identity.

"…Okay," I said. "I understand, but I don't like it. I don't like this rigidity. It's inhuman."

"Perhaps," he replied, then opened his car door. "But that's the price of freedom."

He shot me one last look before getting in. The engine started and the car disappeared into a stream of traffic.

I turned my attention to the dent that the cop's boot had left.

Wait a second – the dent was the familiar one that was near the fuel cap, the one I recognised my brother's ute by. This could only mean one thing: when I had climbed back down from the roof, I landed in the past. A week or so before the dent was made. This knowledge liberated me a little because I understood that the cop could not do anything new to me. He couldn't inflict anything on me that hadn't already happened in the future – he couldn't deviate from the timeline.

Everything was happening too fast. When I got home I received a phone call. People answer their telephones.

I picked it up. "Hello?"

"Louie Trad?" It was a man's voice – a strong tenor.

"Yes. Who's this?"

"Listen carefully. My name's Hercules. I'm a big fan."

"Did you say Hercules?"

"That's right. I saw you up on the roof about a week ago. You were amazing!"

"What is it with the bloody roof?"

"I suggest you don't do it anymore, though – at least for now. You might attract attention from the police."

"I already have. Who did you say you were?"

"Well I can't say too much on the phone, but I represent a group who is sympathetic to people in your, uh, position."

"An organisation?"

"More like an organism. Listen, can we meet?"

"Why?"

"I may be able to help you."

"With what? And for what?"

"All this can be discussed when we meet. I just want you to know that however difficult things get, there are always allies."

"Okay. ...Where?"

"I'm two blocks over from you. I'll move a pot plant as a sign. ...Shall we say in an hour?"

"Okay." And with that we both hung up.

I paced for awhile trying to work out the smartest way to handle this. In the end I decided I didn't want any more trouble in my life than I already had. I wasn't going to prison for anyone – cops or revolutionaries.

Funny enough, Hercules didn't call again.

In the meantime, I decided to continue with my walks. The roof had blown my previous assumptions of reality out of the water, so to speak, but it attracted too much attention. My walks, however, looked perfectly harmless. In truth they were quite the opposite. My particular method ran like this:

As I strolled the block, I watched myself much like a movie. This included watching my emotions and thoughts. The observation caused a separating of Louie into parts. For example, if I can view my mind and its thoughts, it follows on that I am not my mind. An eye cannot see itself. 'I' – the point of consciousness – unattached itself and became freed of the mind. The point of consciousness seemed to reside in Louie's head, as if that was where a 'window of access' resided between planes. I imagined it (my self) as a little white flame.

So, with willpower, 'I' observed Louie's three parts (physical, emotional and mental) while he walked the streets. Keeping this up took a great strain of concentration, and caused the flame to blaze brighter. Eventually it focussed into a point, like the sharp beam in a magnifying glass. The rays gradually broke down the cloud of thoughts that surrounded Louie's head. I called this technique 'Playing the Watcher'.

One day my older brother walked in as I played the Watcher at home. "What are you doing Louie?" he asked.

"I am not Louie." I made Louie say that, like a marionette, shaping the words with his lips in perfect pronunciation.

"Well I'm off to the shop. When you see Louie," said my brother, sarcastically, "ask him if he wants anything."

"Any questions you have for me should be addressed to my marionette. I call it 'Louie'."

"Sure thing, Split-arse," said my brother.

Then I felt a gathering of force. Meditation is like boiling water; if you keep the flame on consistently, it eventually causes the change of state. I felt like the centre of a spinning tornado, as if my crystallised personality was breaking up and the pieces caught in a whirlwind. A tension blazed in my head and the point between my eyebrows buzzed.

But it was only a glimpse. I lost it when Louie came to life and said, "Yes, man, bring me back some hundreds-and-thousands cookies so I can dip them into my tea."

One area that desperately needed the Watcher was Louie's work. It was a place of overbearing monotony. Louie ran through the same routine every single shift on autopilot. The only aspect of work he could recollect clearly was an aching feeling in his legs and feet, and a heavy fatigue. Everything else to do with work was like a half-remembered dream.

What Louie did not know at the time was that the reason every working day was so identical was that it was, in fact, the same day replayed over and over.

When Louie first got the job of steward, he was taken around the hotel and shown which floors to mop, where to take the garbage, the procedure for using the big industrial dishwasher and so forth. After a week he picked everything up and was able to perform his job like textbook. The first day in which that was achieved was then separated and copied. That is to say: that eight-hour chunk of time was copied and pasted to every shift Louie worked.

The timeline was doctored – put on a loop. Every time Louie went through the door into work, he went back in time to that exact day. Crossing the threshold was all that was needed.

After that, Louie could sit back and ride the past, so to speak, because he'd already lived that day.

If I (the abovementioned flame) had been paying attention at work, I would have realised that Louie's hairstyle changed instantly to what it was when he first got the job, and that he had the same argument with the same person about the same subject every single shift. Another similarity was that on the Original Day, Louie became impatient towards the end of the shift because he had to do a half-hour overtime. So, every single time the shift was replayed, Louie's anxiety returned.

This reusing of old time was merely the next step in the industrial revolution. It was very labour effective. However, it was just like reusing videotape over and over, continually taping over the same videocassette caused the quality to deteriorate … and finally cease playing altogether.

Whenever I am Louie, I am unhappy and vulnerable, like lowering myself into a tumultuous river. Salvation comes only in 'retreating to higher ground'.

Louie's eyes always look glazed over, his black irises out of focus, much like someone fatigued or under hypnosis.

On Louie's day off he goes over to the building that all the young people jump from. He isn't committed to anything – he's just sussing out every option.

It is an abandoned building, which is why the kids use it. They hang out on all the floors in gangs smoking drugs, skateboarding and spray painting.

As Louie approaches he falls in step with a teenage girl. They enter the building and ascend the stairs. Lying around the steps is a gang of brutes. They are all warped and bumpy as if made of play-dough … mumbling at each other in a backward language. Louie and the girl step carefully through the teenage minefield and onto the next floor. They enter the creaky lift and wait as it rumbles to the roof.

"You going to jump?" Louie asks.

"That's right," she says defiantly.

"What for, if you don't mind me asking?"

"Because I've got the guts! Are you going to try and talk me out of it?"

"Nope."

"I'm fucking pregnant. I can't go back home and my ex-boyfriend wants me to get an abortion. I can't do that. I would never do that. I should never have gotten with that prick in the first place, but you know how it is with relationships…"

"I'm nobody's saviour."

She looks at Louie. "What's that supposed to mean?"

"Don't expect me to talk you out of suicide."

"I'm not committing fucking suicide!"

"But you said you were jumping!"

"Not to fall; to fly."

"What?"

"Man, don't you know anything? That's what we do here."

"You can't just decide to fly."

"Don't fucking tell me what I can't do! It's just a matter of willpower. The whole universe is the result of willpower. This oppressive society wills us not to fly."

"Then what was all that about being pregnant?"

"Simple. If you are going to attempt something as extreme as flying, you have to have nothing to lose in case you fail. My life is fucked up – I've got nothing to lose but trouble."

They are now on the top of the building, standing on the edge. It's a long way down … but a good day for flying.

The girl looks Louie in the eyes. "I have a feeling I'm going to be the first to succeed!"

She takes a deep breath and with a wild smile she jumps…

She flaps her arms all the way down, where her head splatters against the pavement in a red blossom, tinged with streaks of blonde hair. Her body poses, framed in blood.

Three days later it occurs to Louie why the girl failed: First of all, waiting until you have nothing to lose before making the attempt is a blatant act of faithlessness. A confident act would be jumping when life is good. Just like a selfless act would be giving away your last twenty dollars -- if you can easily afford it you haven't really made a sacrifice. Secondly, thinks Louie: the girl wanted to fly but she reached the top of the building by elevator. Subconsciously, she must have believed she couldn't fly.

Armed with this new reasoning, Louie makes it back to the building. The play-dough characters are still there, moping about. He looks up – it's about eight stories high.

Louie steps back for a clear view of the scene. He pays attention to outlines – where everything begins and stops – the borders of reality. The building ceases sharply and the sky begins. The teenagers are less sharp – their limbs fade out of focus and blend with each other. Their heads, too, are smudged in the sunlight.

Louie considers this illusion and looks for the loophole. He comprehends that everything here is intertwined. His stress is the world's stress. So, in exhaling and relaxing, the world's tension eases correspondingly. The building and the sky react to each other like two liquids – a bubble of brick drifts into the sky, and some bubbles of sky cross the outline into the brick, creating air bubbles in the building.

Louie decides to launch – he lifts from the road and lets himself drift up on the present current of reasoning. Some of the road follows him up in a smoky swirl...

Louie cruises along over the traffic now. He swerves over traffic lights and rooftops. The wind whistles in his ears and smudges moisture from his eyes over his cheeks. For a moment he inhales the new air...

Okay, he thinks, this is my suburb. Bring it down gently.

He lets himself fall a bit, rears to the side and takes out a garbage bin. Dogs begin to bark all over the suburb. He stands up and brushes himself off.

"Okay," Louie says and inspects the houses in front of him. "Which one is my home?" His brother's ute is nowhere to be seen. This will be tricky, he thinks. All the houses have corrugated iron roofs, well-kept lawns, and orange-grey bricks...

He flips a coin and makes a choice, then strides confidently into the yard in front of him and opens the front door. As he steps into the lounge room he knows instantly that this is not his home.

"I'm glad you came," a woman's voice says.

She's sitting on the couch, her eyes like clear blue sky, a sharp angular face and a small-framed body. She wears long sleeves, a high collar and a dark skirt that trails down to her ankles with a picture of a golden cross with a red rose entwined in it. Her hands are linked on her lap.

"I'm sorry," says Louie. "I must have accidentally –"

"There are no accidents," she says.

"Look, I don't even know you."

"I'm Hercules."

Her words feel like a wind. He reels and falls.

"Are you all right?" asks the woman, standing over him. "Let me help you up."

"Get away from me," he snaps, climbing to his feet. "You're not Hercules! Do you think I'm stupid?"

"I am."

"Hercules is a man. I spoke to him on the phone."

She rolls her eyes. "Louie! You should know better than to trust your telephone!"

Louie thinks it over. "Either way. I didn't come to see you. It was just a coincidence."

"Nonsense. You were attracted to me on an etheric level. Attracted on an atomic level, I mean. You see, Louie, we're vibrating at the same rate and frequency."

She reaches forward and pulls the shirt off Louie's shoulders. It has the same effect as opening a door to a concert.

"Look," she calls over the music, gesturing toward a mirror.

Louie sees that his bare torso is smudged out of focus because the atoms are vibrating so fast.

"People like us," she explains, "drift naturally together like musical instruments, playing harmonies."

Louie is too dumbfounded to speak.

"Come on," says Hercules. "Let's go sit on the kitchen floor until everyone gets here."

"Someone is coming?"

"It's a full moon tonight," she says, without elaboration.

"But I don't understand," says Louie. "What is it that you people do?"

"We change things. You know: we move pot plants and stuff. I must say, though, your roof antics were something else! I'm impressed!"

Soon people are flooding in the doors and windows, chattering and laughing to each other. Twenty names are thrown at Louie but he catches only a few – "This is Leonard, Uccello, Robinson, Sunday, Hellen, Scoundrel, Sully, Hanna, Betty, Slick…"

They pull their clothes off and toss them to the side, then dance wildly to their own vibrating bodies. Hercules's clothes fall to her ankles. She floats up into the crowd, leaving Louie alone.

It's all a blur. Louie can't make out any detail. There are no faces, no nipples nor bellybuttons – just a smear of various skin colours. He cannot even decipher which one is Hercules, but he can hear her:

"Louie! Come on!"

Caught in the electric atmosphere, Louie slides into the swarm.

A multi-layered voice flows through everyone:

We are citizens of the nation that sits firm in young, quiet minds.
The nation that is fragmented and scattered amongst all others,
Connected by the shiny web of goodwill.

We who stand two inches off the ground,
flying on our enthusiasm,
Who belly laugh at our imperfections, and plod along laughing,
ever forward,
Who gather the waste and refuse, reorganise it,
and release it new again.

And when others turn blindly and stumble into our nation,
they are shocked –
Shocked and malicious also, taking us as their enemy.
But now destined, nevertheless, to become future citizens.

Citizens of goodwill, of the future.
Explorers of the soul!

As he dances along, Louie loses all inhibitions, all borders to himself and his expected behaviour. In other words, I (the Soul) step in and take control … even if only for a moment.

It's not only the people dancing, but their very atoms are moving as well. Soon a scattering of atoms – points of light – let loose and 'mingle' with each other. Fragments of identities swap, mixing and fusing together. From the distance the scene resembles a pointillist painting.

…Again, who am I?

The bodies are coming back together into a melting mass of skin-coloured clay … separating … reforming … all of us are microcosms with a fragment of everything else in each … and Louie is back.

More or less.

3.

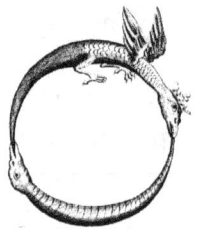

The Announcement

Over the rooftops of an ever-noisy town, the announcement went out. It sounded in every building and over every street and park, but few heard it because the announcement was not spoken out loud. If you'd been there and could hear thoughts, you would have blocked your ears. Almost every mind in the town rambled simultaneously – like a room full of televisions turned on to different channels. Then, of course, there were real televisions and radio signals all joining in the roar. So few people were silent enough to hear what was said, deep in their minds:

"Brothers and sisters. I am speaking on behalf of your more advanced fellows on the Path. Tomorrow will be the beginning of a strange turn in reality and we must adapt if we are to stay in control. Listen closely. As of tomorrow, you will all have but one week to live. That week will then be copied and put on a loop which will last for ten years. Each week within those years will be a replay of the first. This will greatly affect your future, so use your week wisely."

Henry, a man in his twenties, was luckier than most. He'd crashed his motorbike into a fence at the time. In the moments after the crash, he lay stunned underneath the bike, looking up blankly at the stars without a thought in his head. He didn't even remember how he got there.

Then came the announcement.

Henry sensed it intuitively. His mind started again and the meaning of the announcement was sifted through his own capacity for understanding, and then diluted by his own worries and desires. All he sensed was a sudden feeling of mortality, which he attributed to the crash, and the desire to have fun while he was still alive.

He decided that this week he would hit the bars.

When one activity ends and a new activity is yet to begin, the mind briefly returns to the present. So it was with Buddy. The movie he was watching just ended and he turned the television off. He was suddenly very conscious of how silent and lonely it was. And, without realising it, he began to panic about this 'chunk' of time he now had on his hands. During this few-second pause, some of the announcement managed to seep into his consciousness. It swirled around with his feeling of boredom like water and dirt in a glass. He sensed the announcement with a muddy clarity: an inkling that life is repetitious and the feeling of not being able to change things.

It made Buddy feel depressed, so he put on his hat and set out to a friend's house.

Django was playing guitar in a restaurant, improvising around a chord progression and familiarising himself with a particular mode, playing clean and fast. Next to him sat the other two guitarists in the trio, playing the bass and rhythm. Because the guitarists seemed to be in 'the zone', and it was an especially good vibe with the audience, Django played more intensely than usual and concentrated fully on what he was trying to achieve.

His thoughts were replaced by attention to the

music. In the quiet, the announcement slipped into his consciousness. Django went home that night thinking one thing: "I need to practice more."

Helen was meditating during the announcement. She was in her bedroom sitting on a straight-backed chair, eyes closed. Sporadically, and for periods of only a second or two, she managed to quieten her mind, at which time snippets of the announcement seeped in. By the time she opened her eyes the announcement had floated to the surface of her mind in the form of an idea, which she thought was her own. The idea was to organise a schedule for the next week. "If I had only one week to make a difference in the world," she thought, "how would I spend it?" She thought it was strictly theoretical, and wrote a list of things to get done, along with a timetable.

Monday came (Day 1): the reckoning week was upon them. Henry awoke feeling daunted at the prospect of a full week of work. But he showered and got up. Henry worked in the hospitality industry and he didn't start work till the afternoon. So he spent the morning paying bills and shopping. After that, he watched television and drank coffee until it was time for work. After an uneventful evening at work, he knocked off and went straight to the pub with some workmates.

The following day (Day 2), Henry slept in to eleven then more or less repeated the first day. In fact, Monday through to Thursday were practically repeats, as if Monday had been put on a loop. Only it hadn't. Henry looped it voluntarily.

The difference with Friday was that Henry stayed out nightclubbing for much longer. He returned home, with a random party-girl, at three-thirty.

Henry slept until twelve on Saturday. When he awoke, he met with a friend at a café for coffee. Back home at three, then Henry mowed his lawn and did his washing. That evening he saw a movie and had dinner with a group of friends. Afterwards they hit the nightclubs where Henry repeated Friday night.

Sunday (Day 7): Henry slept in. He spent the rest of the day watching television and drinking beer. By the afternoon his previous feeling of needing to break free and party seemed to have exhausted itself, and now Henry felt pacified. He had an early night.

The next day Henry had no control over his actions. As if stuck in a crystallised mould of himself, Henry – although he wasn't altogether aware of it – repeated the previous week right down to every last action, regular as clockwork. For ten straight years.

Buddy spent his week much differently. He didn't work so he slept in every day till about eleven o'clock in the morning. After that, he made himself a lazy breakfast and watched television while he ate. Then he strolled into town, browsed the shops, sat at cafés and read a book. It was a book on fossil fuels and environmental issues.

In the late afternoons he'd usually venture over to one of his friend's houses. There they played computer games or watched DVDs and smoked cigarettes. The only change in this routine was Wednesday night, when he made the leap to attend a community meeting that he'd been thinking about for a long time. The group was focussed on how to deal with climate change and peak oil problems on a local level.

"Can't hurt to turn up and see," he thought hesitantly.

Buddy went fishing with a friend on Saturday morning and played pool at a pub that night. He watched movies on Sunday, smoked cigarettes and played computer games.

That week was then locked in and Buddy's life was set for the next ten years.

Django's week was less ordered. On Monday he got up early because he had to give a guitar lesson. On Tuesday he slept in to ten o'clock, but had to teach guitar at twelve pm through to four o'clock. Wednesday was a day off, but he played a gig that night at a café. Thursday he only taught from nine to eleven but had two rehearsals in the evening. Friday was another day off – with another gig from nine o'clock to eleven at a pub. Saturday he had two gigs straight – one at a café, then afterwards at a pub – where he drank much alcohol. Sunday was for relaxing and practicing...

The thing with Django's week was that in between teaching and doing chores, he usually practiced guitar. In fact, you can safely fill in all the gaps in his days by assuming he was practicing guitar.

That week was then frozen in time and repeated fifty-two times per year for ten years.

Helen wrote a checklist of things she thought needed to be done each day. It included these activities:

Meditation/concentration exercises, morning and evening
Household responsibilities
Study/homework
Exercise
Writing

No matter what day it was, she made sure to get these things done. They didn't take all that long, so there was room enough for leisure time in between. Her days passed into a week, and like the others, her fate was sealed.

The second week, or 'first repeat', went by in ordinary time at the usual speed. However, as the weeks went by, the cycle of Mondays sped up much like someone jumping on a bicycle and starting to pedal – the speed builds and the wheels spin increasingly faster. Soon the spokes cannot be seen at all. In the cycle of the reoccurring week, the days passed by like spokes in a bicycle wheel.

Ten years zoomed by like a roller coaster. It was perceived as no longer than, say, a month.

When it slowed to a halt as quickly as it began, everybody felt a little dizzy and fatigued. They rubbed their eyes as if awaking from a dream, feeling suddenly insecure at their new surroundings; the loop had finished. They had free will.

The end of the ten-year-loop was strangely marked by the fact that many things ended on that day: relationships, careers, degrees in education, etc. It was like the end of one season and the beginning of a new one.

Some people realised straightaway they were in the very same position and state they were in before the ten-year-loop. Nothing had changed … except their age, of course.

Henry found that he had the same job, the same type of friends, the same amount of money and the same amount of skills. He did, however, accumulate some new things. One was that he had a string of ex-girlfriends and lovers and a reputation for that lifestyle. Unfortunately, he was not satisfied. Despite the many affairs he had, Henry still craved night-time company. This included the women, the social scene, and the alcohol. It seemed that he had developed dependence to it.

Henry, unaware of the loop, felt that the last ten years zoomed by so quickly he barely experienced it. Suddenly he was ten years older. Only a roller coaster ride ago he was a young man. Now he was getting too old for the only lifestyle he knew. Society would have it that the older you get the richer you should get. This didn't happen and for the first time Henry felt inadequate.

One thing that was good about the ten-year-loop was that he had no worries – everything just happened. He didn't have to choose and doubt.

Buddy found himself stranded in Suburbia and

in a feeble body. He went into a fit of coughing, his lungs only now registering the tar build-up. On top of his out-of-shape body, he had accumulated some debt. Besides that he had no new skills, no new experiences or money.

Well, actually he did have some new experiences. One of the initiatives of the group that he attended was a community vegetable garden. On that night, Buddy went out with the other volunteers and helped. The loop brought with it many fruits in a more literal sense. This was Buddy's redeeming memory and a fulcrum of enthusiasm. He knew how he wanted to steer the next ten years, and so he got onto the Internet to look up related courses at university. The new day onwards, he volunteered most of his time to the permaculture movement.

Django accumulated many of the usual things too. He had debts, weakened health (from drinking) and his bank balance was roughly the same as before the ten-year-loop.

But one significant thing had changed. Because of all that practising he was now a virtuoso with the guitar. His skill was outstanding. Not only that, but he found that he had an impressive number of recordings and pieces of his own. This excited him and made him want to go play some more. It was also about to excite anybody else who would hear him play – this was the new season about to happen.

Helen found that she had finished her degree and graduated. She was healthy. During the last barely acknowledged ten years, she had written five novels and many more short stories. In addition, the independent magazine she co-edited with her fellow students had become the centre of a movement. This astonished her.

Because of the regular meditations (in the Raja Yoga system), her emotional disposition was much purer than it had ever been. Calmness filled her. She could now attain (though not always) the point of concentration wherein one can hold the attention firmly on Humanity as a 'point of identification,' unhindered by thoughts of the personal self.

The next day, over the rooftops, an announcement sounded. It reached every building and every street and park, but few heard it because the announcement was not spoken out loud. If you'd been there and could hear thoughts, you would have blocked your ears. Almost every mind in the town was rambling simultaneously – like a room full of televisions turned on to different channels. Then, of course, there were real televisions and radio signals all joining in the roar. So few people were silent enough to hear what was said, deep in their minds:

"Brothers and sisters. I am speaking on behalf of your more advanced fellows on the Path. Tomorrow will be the beginning of a strange turn in reality and we must adapt if we are to stay in control. Listen closely. As of tomorrow, you will all have but one week to live. That week will then be copied and put on a loop which will last for ten years. Each week within those years will be a replay of the first. This will greatly affect your future, so use your week wisely."

This time, Helen heard the announcement loud and clear.

4.

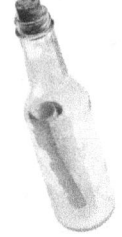

The Wake

I stirred and awoke to find myself seated on the couch. A glorious sun shone through everything, as if my surroundings were translucent. But that effect faded as I awoke.

The television was on and I was alone.

I could not recall how I came to be on the couch, or even what I'd done that day. I continued to watch television, to eat and mope about. At some point I discovered that it was not just that day I couldn't recall, but also many days before.

Just as you begin to forget a dream, I was forgetting my life. The surroundings were familiar (it was my home, after all) but it nevertheless felt new – like reverse deja vu.

So I went to explore the rest of the house, and I found a mirror and stood in front of it. The reflection only seemed vaguely familiar, like an acquaintance as opposed to myself.

This scared me.

Back in the living room I discovered that when I searched through my memory, it felt like looking into the mind of a stranger. My memory wasn't fading after all; it just wasn't mine anymore.

I left the house feeling like a trespasser. Though I didn't notice them at first, two people were on the veranda. They sat silently around a table, so when I saw them I jumped.

One was a Hispanic woman – about fifty years old – and the other was a lean boy of, say, nineteen. According to my memory they were my mother and little brother.

They didn't notice me. Their eyes were glazed over with a shine, and they sat like statues. On further inspection I saw that my brother's foot was tapping so fast that it was a blur. My mother's finger was doing the same speed on the table. They gave off a hum that reminded me of computers on 'standby.'

A wind whooshed by and the door slammed behind me. My family came to life.

"Huh? Leonard, what are you doing?" mumbled

the woman as she looked at me.

"Who's Leonard?" I asked.

"Where are you going, Leonard?" said the boy.

"Oh!" I forced a smile as I realised: "I'm Leonard!"

The boy turned away casually, but the woman's stare intensified. It occurred to me that I might be 'inhabiting' Leonard, because I sure didn't feel like him. I had to get out of there, so I began to walk toward the front gate, sweating under the gaze of the woman who was Leonard's mother. "I'm just going, um, out…" I murmured.

A couple of days later Leonard's family picked me up wandering along the highway. The feeling that I'd recently awakened from another life had persisted all this time. I still felt lazy and I was regularly stretching my arms out and yawning.

The woman who kept saying she was my mother had a solution: to send me on a journey to find a famous doctor. She asked Eddie, her neighbour, to accompany me. Apparently I grew up with Eddie, an Aborigine.

"No worries," he said. "The doc will know what's going on, if anyone does."

Outside the window, I could see the suburban houses huddled around as if to trap me there.

"Let's get on with it," I mumbled.

We said goodbye and climbed into Eddie's Ford. He revved the engine and it slowly left the curb... The tires sank halfway into the cushion-like road, and in the distance the houses rose and fell as if on water. A crowd of homes in front parted to let us through.

"What's going on, Eddie?" I asked as the car pushed its way slowly through the suburbs. I was lost already, but Eddie seemed to know where he was going.

"It's all good," he said, lighting a cigarette. "I went through the same thing last year."

The smoke-ribbon from his cigarette stretched far behind us until I couldn't see the end. After winding through street after street – like the repeated background of a cartoon – I could have sworn that the end of his cigarette smoke was in front of us. "Where are we going?" I asked.

"To find Doctor Livingston."

"Who is he?"

"The only man who'll know what to do."

"Where is he?"

"Some years ago he journeyed deep into the suburbs – the deepest part – and nobody has seen him since."

"He'll understand, then?"

"If he's still alive."

Our homes were not too deep into the suburbs.

The tops of the city's high-rise buildings could still be seen over the horizon. These were beacons, to reassure us. "We're not lost as long as they are still in sight," said Eddie.

Yet Eddie drove away from them. My sense of direction disappeared when the high-rise buildings disappeared under the horizon.

After winding through an endless repetition of streets it was no surprise that I became hypnotised. I don't know how long I was under, but eventually Eddie nudged me and snapped me out of it.

"Look," he said.

The car was parked in a street in front of a non-descript house. Eddie and I got out and joined a group of native Suburbanites on a neatly manicured lawn. They looked up at the roof, where an Indian or Pakistani man stood holding a bottle and a ream of paper. When I squinted at the paper there appeared to be writing on it. As we watched, the man rolled up the paper, shoved it into the bottle and corked it. Then he raised the bottle above his head and let go.

The Suburbanites all applauded as the bottle floated away – upwards – across the town on currents of the air. When the bottle disappeared behind some clouds, the crowd dispersed and the Indian fellow climbed down from the roof.

Eddie and I waited for him on the lawn.

"Doctor Livingston, I presume?"

The doctor was a middle-aged man with a potbelly. He was originally from India. The strange thing is that he also had a boxer's nose, all bent and flat – the reward for giving bad news to patients. He called me into his dank office, which was the spare room of a private house, and sat me opposite him on a hard chair. Eddie remained outside in the garage, which was converted into a waiting room.

When I explained my situation to the doctor he wasn't at all moved. I might have just described to him the common flu.

"...I don't know," I said. "Have you ever woken up one day and wondered how you ended up in this life?"

"Yes, yes, Lenny, very good," he said in a deep voice.

"Leonard."

"Leonard. Sounds common enough. How old are you?"

"Twenty-six."

"A good age. Not a moment too soon. What I want you to do Leonard is to think back to your very first memory and tell it to me."

I searched through the memory again. It was difficult but I finally found that there was no recollection at all before one event: I was on a sled of some sort, though it wasn't snowing. It was on a plateau and the muddy path led down a hill into the sea. It zoomed down faster and faster until all I knew was the feeling of speed. I plunged into the water and the memory ends there. I told it to the doctor.

"Ah yes, very good," he said.

"So what's happening then?"

The doctor told me to stand and lift my shirt. He put a stethoscope on my back and went on through all the usual checkup exercises.

"What you consider to be your identity," said the doctor, "is an accumulation of debris – additions that you have picked up through your life thus far. Are you following me?"

I made no reply.

"Very good," he continued. "Imagine that you are up on the plateau you speak of. This is you as a young child. Your soul is only just taking control of its vehicle, which is, of course, the body. Now you are speeding down the ramp and into an onslaught of influences. It is at this point in your life that you lose sight of yourself, being distracted by all the learning experiences. You then begin to identify with your experiences. Thus you are no longer conscious of yourself as you were – before the experiences – and still are underneath them. And what does no longer being conscious mean?"

"Um, I'm not sure."

"It means being unconscious. That core part of you is asleep. And all the while, the outer identity has kept on building up."

"Go on doctor."

"Now then ... you zoom along under the 'sea-of-unconsciousness', which takes you through your adolescent years, through school right up to high school, then university. And you are running through new experiences along the way. You zoom through university and all the people you've met, and into the work force. The sled/identity is catching more and more debris until you no longer even see the sled. Everything is latching on –

"Suddenly, in your twenties and in the work force, the sled is running out of momentum. It runs out and just drifts ... and presto! You wake up here."

"End of the path?"

"Not quite. Before you the track leads up, out of the water, to yet another plateau. But you have reached what we call the Wake Up Period, which ranges from the mid-twenties to early thirties – depending on the person. Are you following me? Leonard, for many years you have believed you were this accumulation of flotsam. This week you snapped out of it and intuited that you are, in fact, beneath it all. You are awake underwater."

"So I'm not Leonard!" I stood up. Everything I

felt was confirmed.

"Leonard is the name of that collective outer layer of crud."

The doctor smiled and turned towards a set of drawers. He opened one and rummaged through it.

"You're a very cryptic fellow," I said. "But thanks. Now I don't suppose there's anything to be done."

"Oh there is much to be done," he said taking a piece of paper. "That's why I came here to the suburbs."

"Are you kidding me?" The Suburbs are like an elephant graveyard: people only go there to die. Very few people who disappear into the suburbs are ever heard from again. "Why don't you come back to the city with us – back to civilisation?" I suggested. "We need more doctors."

"Oh, I'm not much of a doctor anymore. Not since I woke up." He began to scribble away on the paper with a pen.

"Then what is it that you do out here?"

"I practise magic."

"Magic?"

"The most important thing for us is to rise above the surface of the water and reach that second plateau."

I considered the metaphor... if that's what it was. I couldn't see the connection between that and magic.

"To do this," he continued, while scribbling, "we need to establish a connection with the surface. White magic works vertically."

He took a bottle out of the drawer, went to the window and opened it. "Some woken people become magicians, you see. The others go back to sleep."

"What is that?" I asked, pointing to the paper.

"Your prescription: It is an SOS I am sending to the surface."

The doctor/magician stuffed whatever he'd written into the bottle, corked it and held it out the window. As he let go, he chanted some words that I didn't catch, and then said: "So mote it be!"

The bottle bobbed and floated, and then rose higher and higher into the deep blue sky...

Eddie was seated in the waiting room near two other strangers. The other two sat under a faulty light bulb. As it flickered on and off, the two strangers flickered from Anglo Saxon to Indian.

Eddie stood as I approached and said: "Come on. I'm hanging for a smoke."

From the moment I stepped outside, I was disorientated again. Suburbia stretched out before me in all directions. Eddie led me to his car. He started it up and once again the crowd of houses in front of us parted to let us through. But this time, floating overhead, was a message in a bottle.

In time I began writing SOSs myself. And to write, of course, I needed to 'spell'. I became a magician.

I'm about to roll this story up, stuff it into a bottle and send it adrift. Maybe you'll find it.

5.

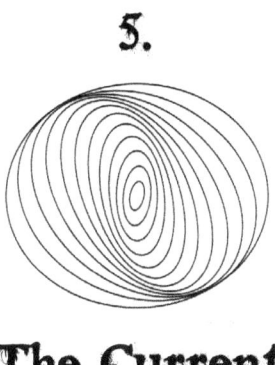

The Current

Imagine that every day, the moment you step outside your front door, a strong current carries you away with it. Around you go to various places, thrown in with other people along the way. You have no control whatsoever; you're simply carried along wherever the current takes you. By the end of the day this stream swings by your home again and drops you off at the front door. You retire until tomorrow's ride. Years later, of course, you've accomplished nothing except age and deterioration.

Meet Oscar. He's a scruffy fellow who shaves once in a while and tries not to waste money on haircuts. The result is shoulder-length tangles of brown hair.

Oscar feels that forces outside of himself commandeer all his time. He feels every lost minute. Is that right Oscar?

"Yeah," he says begrudgingly. "At night I have dreams where I cut myself with some random object and blood gushes out of me in streams."

Oh. So, what happens?

"Well, I stand there in despair, watching my life seep away, until I wake up. The objects are different each time – a coffee cup, a coat button... so forth..." His attention wavers and he gives his sandpaper chin a good scratch.

Oscar – what's the solution to this problem? Got any ideas?

He looks back at us. "Eh? Well hell yes," he says straightening up. "I'm making a solemn vow to, uh, extract at least a few hours of constructive living each day."

I like to think of Oscar as an alchemist of old, trying to extract the elixir from solar rays. To succeed, Oscar has to resist the current. This may sound easy enough...

"Oh it's not easy," Oscar pipes up. "Just making the vow has brought up the many obstacles facing me. Which together, you know, make up the current. Let me show you something."

Oscar reaches into his coat pocket and pulls out

a well-handled piece of paper. He unfolds it and shows it to us. On it is a list:

1. Work
2. Social/Entertainment
3. Family
4. Fitness
5. Aspiration
6. My Thing
7. Sleep

What is this, Oscar?

"I've been, uh, dissecting my life. Here are the parts which make up the whole. The sections."

Can you explain five and six for us?

"Sure. Aspiration is that part of life that you devote to self-development or, uh, improvement. You know, it might mean religion. Could be financial or scientific studies. And so forth."

I see. And your 'Thing'?

"Well," says Oscar breaking into a proud smile. "For me it's the guitar!" He mimes a guitar with his hands. "Your 'Thing' is your chosen mode of expression in, uh, the material world. It could just as well be gardening, you know, or writing or kung fu." His eyes suddenly narrow, and he points at us like Uncle Sam. "Restless is the person who has no Thing…"

It's Oscar's day off work and he's looking forward to some quality living. Resisting the urge to sleep in, he jumps from his bed and heads for the shower. Afterwards, he takes a pen and writes himself another list.

"This one's a checklist," he says overhearing me. "To be completed."

Can we see?

"Sure," he finishes writing and shows us the paper:

- Morning meditation
- Reading Current News
- Household chores
- Guitar practice/ music study
- Physical training
- Study Spanish
- Esoteric study
- Evening meditation
- Music listening

"I'll be writing a checklist each day or so from now on. Scrutinising the first list has led me to find that some of the sections in it are actually obstacles. Three to Six are needed aspects. But I'll tell you, I detest points One and Two."

Work and Social/Entertainment?

"That's right. A person's social life," he decides, "is an addiction. People need company like a junky needs a hit."

What about Work?

"I just don't like my job. Takes a lot of time away, you know. Maybe it'd be different if it were My Thing."

Oscar takes his paper back. "Anyway, I'm busy so I'll talk to you later."

Just as planned, he sits for a good twenty-minute meditation (which fits in to his Aspiration column). Afterwards he sits at the coffee table with a cup of tea and some eggs, while reading a broadsheet rag.

But what's this! Coming up (or should I say 'flowing' up?) the driveway, and heading for the door, is his good friend Giwi. He knocks on the door and Oscar saunters over to answer it.

"How are you there, Giwi?"

Giwi is a broad shouldered fellow with a mop of black hair that hides his eyes. "I'm not bad at all," he says. "And yourself?"

"Can't complain," Oscar says, and he leads Giwi inside where he shares his pot of tea.

"I'm heading home to meet Scotty," Giwi says as he drinks. "We're going to play some computer games and maybe have a feed. Are you in?"

Oscar shoots us a quick glance. He gives his chin a good scratch. "I've a few things that need doing," he says.

"Oh," says Giwi. "So you're too busy?"

"Of course," continues Oscar, "I don't need to begin my tasks right away…"

"Are you in or not?"

"Yes," says Oscar, giving Giwi a friendly slap on the shoulder. "Yes I am."

He finishes his tea and steps into the current. Off they go….

Hours later Oscar is seated on Giwi's couch with Scotty and Giwi. They're playing computer games and drinking coffee. Oscar doesn't look so happy.

"Socialising is like a siren's song, luring you to drown your minutes," he grumbles.

He begins to pass when it's his turn on the game. He fidgets on his chair. He gets up and paces.

Goddamnit, he thinks. A kingdom for a guitar! If only Giwi had one around – I could work on some stuff. I've got to get back home and practice. And, shit, I haven't cleaned the house – my folks'll be pissed off!

Finally, after passing on his turn again, Oscar decides the only option is to catch a bus home. He can make it back in less than forty minutes – then the whole day won't be lost.

The doors swing open and the current floods into the room, carrying three men in: Oscar's friends Lee, Luke and Ben.

"Hey fellas!" says Ben. "Who's up for the cinema?"

"What are you going to see?" asks Giwi.

As they discuss it, Oscar knows he must act now. Saying goodbye, he pushes against the current and out the door.

After a torturously long bus ride home where he feels every lost minute, Oscar closes the door behind him and sighs.

"Okay," he says. "Time to clean the house!" He does so, and an hour later he's finished. The clock says three-twenty. "I still have time to practice," he says and heads for his bedroom.

But look – here comes the current again, sweeping up the driveway. There's a knock at the door.

"For fuck sake!" Oscar cries. He puts his guitar down and answers the door.

Lola, his girlfriend, stands there looking mighty fine.

"Lola," he says. "Hello."

"Hi," she says. "What are you up to?"

"Well, nothing much. Practicing a little guitar."

"Want to get some ice-cream?"

At first he resists, but then her eyes twinkle under her long lashes. He feels himself floating away with her, as if on a raft….

"Where shall we eat it?" Lola asks as they stand in the ice-cream shop.

"Right here's fine by me," says Oscar. He licks his mango-flavoured scoop and the heaviness in his stomach reminds him that it's almost exercise time.

"No, no, no," she laughs. "This won't do. Let's go to the esplanade and watch the sunset!"

Fuck the sunset, Oscar thinks. I haven't exercised in three days. My muscles don't feel tight, my stomach sags and I'm eating shit food! But I can't say this to her – after all, it's not her fault. Reluctantly, and forcing a smile, he answers: "Okay. Sure."

They stroll towards the esplanade at corpse speed while Lola chitchats about subjects that fit into the Social Life section. When she finally changes the subject, she talks about subjects that fit into the Work section.

"You seem a little bit aloof today," she says, looking at him with her big hazel eyes.

"Do I?" asks Oscar. "I don't mean to."

At the esplanade they find a park bench to sit on. With her head on his shoulder, Oscar and Lola watch the colourful sky as the sun inches towards the horizon.

Hurry fucking up, thinks Oscar. Sink! Sink! Piss off below the horizon! How long does it bloody take? I have to go and practice guitar! (He has decided that Aspiration, Family and Fitness will have to be sacrificed to make way for My Thing, the guitar.)

"Beautiful, isn't it?" says Lola.

"Sure is," Oscar says through gritted teeth. "Look at those colours."

Oscar arrives home with a scowl. His eyebrows are knitted with a tension almost strong enough to tear a black hole.

"Hey son," calls his mother from the living room. "Come and join us! There's a good movie on the telev–"

"Go to hell," he yells, slamming his bedroom door and taking up his guitar. Although his fingers shiver with rage, he tries to warm up. Then he stops. I have to be up at six for work tomorrow, he thinks. Depression sets in.

I'm in no state to practice. I've lost my morale. And I've gone and insulted my family. What I need to do now is accept that the day is lost. Indeed – another day is lost forever and with nothing accomplished. Defeated, he goes to the living room and watches television with his mother, sister and brothers.

A dream: Oscar's dead father is on a ladder, against a high cabinet. Oscar stands at the foot of the ladder. His father searches the top shelf, which holds large brown pitchers. He finds the pitcher with the word 'Oscar' written on it.

"Here," he calls down. "Hold out your hands."

Oscar does so, as if to catch something.

His father picks the pitcher up. "Now pay attention, son. This is all I can give you." He tips the pitcher upside down, pouring clear liquid out.

Oscar tries frantically to catch the liquid as it spills through his hands onto the floor.

The next day Oscar decides that things will be different. Today, as it turned out, is his rostered day off work. Oscar is determined to resist the current. Just like yesterday, he wakes up and heads for the shower. Next, he meditates for twenty minutes and feels absolutely poised – ready for the struggle. He crosses meditation off his checklist. Breakfast time, and, right on queue, here comes the current: the telephone rings.

"Hello," says Oscar.

"Oscar! It's Ben."

"How are you, Ben?" The current flows through the receiver and into the room. Oscar feels the pull as it moves toward the door. He grabs hold of the couch.

"I'm alright. Still breathing, I s'pose," says Ben. "Listen, what're you doing?"

"Nothing much."

"Wanna go get a coffee in town? I'm bored."

"Um…well…actually, I think I'll give it a miss today. I have some chores to do and I wanted to get some guitar practice in."

"Fair enough. You're coming out tonight though?"

"Tonight?"

"We're all going on the town for drinks."

"I'll see."

"Alright. You'd better. We miss you, Osc'. I'll see you later, yeh?"

"Yeh, we'll see," Oscar replies distractedly.

Looking up, he finds himself outside the front door. The current has dragged the couch out and onto the veranda. "Whoa!" he cries as the current continues down the street, dragging leaves and pulling other people out of their houses.

Oscar holds his ground and successfully resists the first assault. It passes completely until there is no breeze whatsoever, and the air feels heavy and stagnant. It is dead quiet, with houses like gravestones as far as the eye can see. And just to rub it in – a senior citizen hobbles by on a walking frame.

Oscar turns to us: "You know how it feels?" he asks. "It's like driving your car for miles and then suddenly getting out and walking. Everything has slowed right down." He about-turns, goes back inside and hangs the phone up.

Later, Oscar is in his room, seated with his guitar. He begins to warm his fingers up with old repertoire. After five minutes of this, he starts on one of the pieces he is currently working on. Concentration is difficult, however, as his mind keeps wandering to where the current is. I wonder whom it's picked up, and where it's taking them, he thinks.

He puts his head down and concentrates.

Another five minutes go by … and guess who is at the door?

"Hi, Lola," says Oscar.

"Hi. Not interrupting anything, am I?" Lola is here with her friend, Samantha.

"Hey there," says Samantha.

"Hello. I'm just practicing guitar."

"Cool." The girls step past Oscar and into the living room. "Don't mind us, then. We're just going to use your place to colour our hair."

"Okay. What colour?"

"I'm going for black, and Samantha likes orange. What do you think?"

"Hmmm. Yeah, I think they'll look wicked." He turns towards the bedroom. "Don't mind me, okay. I'm just in here, on the guitar."

"Okay."

Ten more minutes and Oscar is making ground.

But as he practices his fingering in a particularly difficult phrase, he hears the girls giggle to each other. He also hears the television. He ignores them and continues ... but just as he does, his bedroom walls turn transparent. In fact, everything in the house is transparent except for the outer walls, the television, and the two girls.

Oscar tries not to look at them as they giggle and gossip. He tries not to watch the television. "For fuck sake!" he grumbles.

But he continues practicing guitar. In the background Samantha is fiddling with Lola's hair. One moment it is green, the next blue ... then it is red, and then yellow and so on. Every time the colour changes, they hold up a mirror and giggle. And the current swirls around them blowing their hair up.

Oscar pays louder.

Perhaps an hour later, Oscar puts the guitar down and glances through the wall at the girls. One has golden hair, the other silver. They are in their underwear. But the living room seems far away now – kilometres away.

Scratching his chin, he says: "Look, I've been following the current for so long, that being outside of it feels desolate. This well-spent time has mentally tired me – I'm not used to so much concentration. I need a rest."

Feeling happy that he has at least used an hour well, Oscar puts his guitar down and heads for the living room. He finds the girls fully clothed. One has black hair, and the other orange.

Oscar is in a car speeding towards the city, when he feels the guilt again. He is crammed in the back seat with Lola, Samantha and Scotty. Giwi is driving and Ben has 'shotgun.'

For fuck sake, thinks Oscar, there goes another wasted day. All I seem to do is kill time. And these bastards won't ever take no for an answer. I should move to a goddamn desert where I can be alone.

The current swings the car into a parking lot, and then sweeps everybody out of the car. They are now on the main street where all the nightclubs are.

Oscar feels the united anticipation of the people. They can't wait to be in the clubs with a drink in their hands.

Oscar's brows knot up again. I've missed out on training yet again. I'm going to miss the evening meditation. I've done no study. And how much money am I going to blow on drinks? He wants to leap from the stream. But he can't – Lola is holding his hand. He is chained to the current.

In a club now and Oscar ends up buying the first round of drinks. He knows that if he drinks a lot, his frustration will be magnified and he will become disorderly. So he makes sure to nurse one scotch. Everybody is discussing which club or pub to go next; the current is never satisfied – it always wants to be one step into the future.

I'm tired of being anxious, Oscar thinks. He waits for the right moment, when Lola and his friends are on the dance floor, then slips out into the street. A river of people flows down the footpath. Oscar pushes against the current, towards a taxi depot.

In a taxi, Oscar checks his wallet. It will be the first weekend that he hasn't spent over fifty dollars. He smiles.

The taxi turns off the main road and out of the stream. Oscar feels relieved immediately as a wave of vertigo instantly slows everything down. The driver, who is a Chinese bloke, must feel it too, as he moans – "Unnnghh!"

Oscar sighs: the desire to be one step into the future has disappeared. Everything is slower, and oh, so peaceful.

The second Oscar steps out of the taxi, it springs back towards the city as if it were on a rubber band. Standing in his yard, Oscar looks towards the city. He can hear and see what he is missing out on – like watching a distant storm. His hands shake, and a craving for the current returns. Oscar suddenly feels very depressed, like he's the only person in the entire suburbs tonight. Proving him wrong, however, a senior citizen hobbles by on a walking frame.

Oscar performs his night meditation, and, to his surprise, it completely purges him of the craving. He opens his eyes in a state of contentment. Meditation had been a duty to him before, theoretical and tedious in nature. Now he has experienced an aspect of its power.

I feel like playing guitar, he smiles. And by the time he finishes practicing, it's three in the morning. Tired and satisfied, he sleeps.

Oscar continues like this – a victory here, a defeat there – on his path towards performing the perfect day. He causes many problems along the way (Lola was upset that he left the club without a word) but each day gets slightly better than the last.

If we view his life in fast-forward we will see an almost repeating cycle of events and places, gradually merging into the perfect pattern. This pattern, like Fibonacci's spiral, or a perfectly timed breathing exercise, continually builds – gathering power.

But Oscar hasn't achieved his full power yet. He still foresees adjustments, and he hasn't entirely extinguished his desire for 'group procrastination'.

Though his daily checklists are still not regularly completed, his chief achievement so far is an established, non-negotiable four-hour practice each day. When he rehearses with his musician friends, he finds that he is fast surpassing them in capability.

He feels good about his improvement, but he is beginning to foresee something that disturbs him: a period of solitude. If the snowball effect continues, he will have nobody to call his peer, nobody who lives a lifestyle congruous to his own – and, thus, nobody who will completely understand him. Oscar is already spending less and less time with his friends.

One day, in an attempt to retain a confidant, Oscar leaps into the current and speeds towards Lola. He calls this 'Operation Snatch'. Like a skydiving stuntman, Oscar zigs and zags down the current towards Lola, dodging countless people.

He closes in with arms outstretched, sweeps in and latches on to her.

"Oscar!" she exclaims. "To what do I owe this…?"

"Don't ask questions, baby!" he says. "Just hold on tight and trust me!"

He rears to the edge of the current, taking her with him.

"Oh my!" Lola exclaims.

Oscar takes a deep breath, and leaps from the current. They land in a stunt roll and slide to a halt. The couple are sprawled in the middle of a bitumen road. Time has stopped. There is no wind and the silence is deafening. Houses are lined up like tombstones for as far as the eye can see.

Oscar stands and dusts himself off. He helps Lola up. She rubs her eyes and looks around.

"What is this?" she asks. Her voice echoes throughout the suburbs.

"This is the world outside the current," he says.

"What current?"

"I think its name is Desire."

She turns in every direction to get a feel of the place.

"Well," says Oscar. "What do you think?"

"This is a shit hole," she says.

"That's because we're never here to maintain it."

She breaks out in a sweat and her hands are shaking. "I'm bored, Oscar. Get me to a radio. Quick!"

"We don't need to," he says. "We can listen to the sounds around us."

"Come on! Let's go see a movie."

"But we are in one. You and I are the main characters! What say we make it interesting?"

"I agree. Let's make it interesting and go see a

movie."

"But Lola…"

"I need to get to the Internet."

"Lola! Don't you see? The current isn't real."

"What fucking current? Oscar, you have to come down to the real world. Here – have a splif and relax, for goodness sake!" Lola produces a marijuana joint and lights up. Oscar turns it down. "Whatever," says Lola.

As Oscar watches, Lola fades away in a kaleidoscope of green smoke. He catches glimpses of her in the distant current at various bends and turns. His eyes glisten with moisture as a senior citizen hobbles by on a walking frame.

Now, bear with me. I want to dissect Oscar so that you can see how I – the narrator – see things.

I see Oscar as a three-tiered being: physical, emotional and intellectual. Retreat inwards for a moment, behind Oscar's brain, to his emotions, then behind his emotions to his mind, and further inwards along the golden thread of life … until we arrive at his soul – me, in other words!

Hello there.

I have the appearance of a little golden Oscar.

From back here, in a little place deeper even than thought, I lean forward on my throne and scrutinise Oscar. My chin is propped on one hand

and my eyes are squinting. Come on and pan around behind me, so you can see what I see.

Ah! Very interesting: I do not see one Oscar, but no less than seven different Oscars – one for each of the seven sections or parts of his life. They each exist at the same time yet in separate time frames.

Nice one, says I. Everything seems to be coming along.

I pull out a handkerchief and wipe my forehead. Phew! I say. But it sure is hard work to keep my eye on seven external mes at once! Not even a DJ has seven records going! What to do?

In order to help my creative process, my throne changes into a toilet seat. And presto! – I have an idea. I have to find a way to combine sections! I'll integrate these Oscars into one being.

One idea leads to another: Say! If I can pull them into one Oscar, he may just be strong enough to hold me! I'll be able to go right on down to the physical plane and animate him. Then – budda-bing, budda-boom – think of the changes I could make.

I like this idea. Leaping forward in what looks like a karate stance, I simultaneously thrust both arms forward so that lightning-like missiles fly from the tips of my pointed fingers. Seven missiles, each containing the new idea, zoom towards the seven Oscars. I watch with hawkeyes to see if they reach their target, which is, of course, the brain.

Missile One crosses into the mental plane and zooms into Oscar's mental body (mind). So far, so good.

But there is a 'meteor field' up ahead! Oscar's old ideas and biases are lingering in his mind like a herd of dark clouds.

The missile tries to dodge, but soon its way is blocked. It crashes and fragments. Some of the fragments make it to the emotional body, where they are lost in the waves.

Damnit!

Missile Two bursts through into the mind with as much vigour as Missile One. The thought forms rear up to block the way...

Oh no!

But the missile is quick! It zooms through a gap and increases its lead on the thought forms.

It's clear!

Still on target, Missile Two heads out towards the emotional tier. It bursts through into Oscar's emotional body...

In appearance, the emotional body is like a waterbed that is shaped like an upright person – in this case Oscar. If Oscar gets emotional or loses his temper over something in the physical plane, the emotional body breaks out in waves.

That is what must have happened because

Missile Two has been thrown off course. It circles around the emotional body a few times before it rears into a tailspin and is lost.

But not all is lost. Missile Three makes it through the emotional body, and so does Missile Seven – right through to the sleeping Oscar's brain. They explode into white light and the soul's idea is registered in Oscar's consciousness.

We cross back to Oscar's perspective now. He awakes one morning, sits up in bed and says: "Eureka! I have an idea!"

How does one combine sections?, ponders Oscar. His first inclination is to take a look at his two most disliked sections, Work and Social/Entertainment. Reduce the bastards – that's if I can't get rid of them!

And so...

Work. How do I integrate Work into another section? And which section?

Answers flood forth: first, he decides to save his money. Up till now, Oscar would spend all his money by the next payday.

He begins saving, and this fits into his Aspiration section. As time goes by he has money stashed away to invest in a musical venture or help his family. The Family section!

And so on flow the ideas. Next he thinks of the

Social/Entertainment section. Combine that with Fitness and Aspiration, and, of course, My Thing. Eliminate social relationships based solely around killing time, strengthen social relationships based on learning, supporting and creating.

Gradually the seven sections shrink to five. The soul's out-flowing power, correspondingly, becomes more concentrated, creating bonus energy all around. Each section steps up in intensity, to their next respective levels. Oscar's strength of presence, physical and otherwise, is noticeable on sight.

But all of a sudden it all comes to a halt – as another obstacle surfaces. Oscar is rehearsing in a band when without warning he stops playing and puts his guitar down.

"What are you doing?" asks the bass player.

"I'm scatterbrained," says Oscar. He stands up and rubs his fists in his eyes.

"Want skip move the to song and we'll you to next on this?"

Oscar's brain is overheated. It takes in the words but cannot yet extract any meaning. It slowly computes the sentence…

You to this and we'll skip want song next to the one move?

…computing…

You want to skip this move and next song one

we'll on to?

…computing…

"Oscar?" calls the band.

…computing…

Complete: You want to skip this one and we'll move on to the next song?

Oscar looks back and says, "Um…no. I think I need to go and get some rest."

He walks out the front door.

The band call after him: "Hey! Matter guitar? Oscar the what's don't lift about idiot need alright a be an you're!"

Oscar does not compute this. His brain is so hot right now that he is afraid to set it to work on anything. Steam hisses from the pores on his head, and from his ears. One more degree hotter and Oscar is sure his head will catch fire.

So he sticks to the shade all the way home.

Let the mind wander, he thinks. Whatever you do – don't concentrate!

His jaw drops, his eyes are glazed, his arms reach out as he blunders home like the town drunk. Heart racing, he makes it to the couch – and to the comedy channel on television. Phew! Like a mobile telephone hooking up to a charger, Oscar's eyes and mind hook up to the television.

…RECHARGING…TEMPERATURE DROPPING…

A week later Oscar comes to. He finds himself watching a movie at a friend's house. I must have drifted here on the current, he thinks. He gets up and makes his way home.

Refreshed again, Oscar thinks over what has happened: It seems that rest is a needed part of the cycle. The Social/Entertainment section should be included, but the title should be changed to Recharge. It should not be overindulged in, nor taken away – balance, in other words.

One night on Recharge, Oscar is at a pub with his friends. Through the drinking and talking, Oscar gets a glimpse into the mechanics of his friends' lives. For instance, not everyone includes seven sections. A more common layout is:

1. Work
2. Recharge
3. Family

Scotty's is only Recharge and Family. Giwi's is only Work and Recharge. You can imagine the possible variations.

Suddenly a missile of white light explodes in Oscar's brain.

Hmm, he thinks. Combining and reducing sections is not necessarily good. Reducing can be counterproductive. The important thing, I think, is to imbue every section with a fragment of the

Aspiration section.

Oscar is giving a solo performance. He is seated, in an uptown suit, with a classical guitar propped on one knee.

Retreating inwards again, we find that his emotional body is still. Further in, the mind is also still – poised to do the soul's bidding. Inwards again and you see me. I am on my feet, with my arms around a huge fire hose. The hose originates from somewhere even further inwards. I aim the nozzle outwards – towards Oscar's brain. Then I glance over my shoulder and yell, Okay! Turn her on and let her rip!

The hose jerks around for a second, and then whoosh! White light, like water, comes gushing out, and jets towards the physical world.

It flows through the mental body – cleaning out all the stagnant thought forms. Then through the emotional body into the brain, down Oscar's nerves, into his fingers...

Oscar begins the concert. The first piece is Asturius by Isaac Albeniz, a fast and furious score. He attacks the guitar like a passionate love scene, or a fight to the death. The power flows through Oscar and, using the music as a conductor, jumps across space to the audience.

Everybody tenses as the power hits and enters them.

From a distance, the building lights up with a brilliant aura. As the dying plants in the yard come to life, a senior citizen throws away his walking frame and runs to the building.

By mid-concert, the magnetism rivals even the current, and thus pulls people out of it – towards the concert.

On the emotional level all the souls in the concert hall fire white missiles out towards their personalities.

The next day, Oscar stands in his yard and looks over the beautiful suburbs. Everything seems harmonious. In the distance he sees the current like a giant, winding snake. His neighbours are already returning to it. He sighs.

He turns to us and says: "You know, I don't crave the current at all anymore."

And then a thought pops into his head: a woman's naked body, smooth and rocking with curves.

"Oh no," says Oscar. In the past he had Lola. But he's single now, and the craving is making his hairs (not to mention his penis) rise and point to the distant current. The next image is of Lola's twinkling eyes, pulling him closer...

He lifts his snout towards the current, and, nostrils flaring, takes in the scent of women. Drool streams from his now pointed teeth.

It's not over yet.

6.

Suburban Army Reserve

It is too bright but gradually things become clear and you soon see that you are standing naked at a dinner party. But don't worry: you discover that as long as you move slowly, nobody notices you. Whenever you make sudden movements, it's as if you become visible. So you float along slowly through the party like a ghost. You poach a glass from the waiter, who carries a tray of them. The wine tastes sad.

In a full-length mirror, you catch a glimpse of yourself: you're female. Your nipples poke out, giving the impression that they are searching for someone or something.

The music is slow and pulsing. The whole room

vibrates to it. You cannot resist moving to the dance floor. As you dance, your breasts separate from you and float around nearby, like water balloons.

People start to notice you. You close your eyes and keep moving but you feel very embarrassed. The head waiter comes by and announces: "Oh yes, beautiful, isn't she? This is our 'living sculpture'. Floating limbs variety. She loves music." Everyone claps.

On the other side of the room, you see your first love … as he or she was back then, and your breasts drift across the room towards him/her. S/he sees them and grabs one. S/he seems to have mistaken your nipples for bottles and loosens the nipple on one to take a drink. You feel s/he sucking it all down intensely, which causes you to rock around. People start to laugh.

Look over your shoulder – see that door? Make for it.

The next room is full of your old friends. Some are from school and some are relatives. Some are compositions of people you've known and still know. They're all deformed in one way or another: Some are missing legs and walking with crutches, others have only one arm.

"We've certainly come a long way," says an ex-associate that you've never liked. He looks like a corpse, but is dressed in a very expensive suit. His eyes are little spotlights and you avoid them, so as not to be seen naked.

"How'd this happen?" you ask your best friend.

He or she smiles, revealing missing teeth, and says: "It's alright. Nobody's perfect. When I burn my body I get high on the fumes."

Your best friend stands next to the window and his/her skin starts burning in the sunlight. The smoke rises and fogs up the room. Everyone breathes it in and gets high. They're smiling madly like at a drunken party, but their eyes flow with tears.

Your best friend starts to wither away. For God's sake, don't just stand there – tell them to get away from the window!

Your best friend doesn't listen. His/her clothes dissolve and you begin to see the bones underneath the skin. The fumes are pink now and everyone is sexually aroused. Your friend is moving to his/her death like a stripper. Everyone dances erotically.

A door bursts open and a soldier charges in. He starts blasting everyone to pieces with a machine gun, clearing the room. You crouch down and cover your ears.

Soon, you are standing in dusty rubble, as if the people were all made of concrete.

"LISTEN UP!" the soldier screams at you. As

he does the whole room vibrates like a stereo. "YOU ARE A SOLDIER! STOP MESSING AROUND – REPORT TO BARRACKS AND AWAIT YOUR ORDERS!"

A painting of the barracks is on the wall. You sense that in order to get there you need to abstract yourself away from your own image. So stare at the painting now (oils), and try to identify yourself as a solder in the army of the Forces of Goodness, a completely different person than yourself.

The old you – the woman – is now staring at you from outside the painting, but the core you is now in the painting. You are now a soldier – and also a man, unshaven and with knotted, greasy hair. Your uniform is unbuttoned and underneath it your white singlet is stained with food. Looking around, you notice that the so-called barracks looks exactly like ordinary working-class suburbia, but loafing about on the verandas and strolling along the fence lines are soldiers, all unkempt and half dressed.

You look at your papers to see what number house you are assigned to. It has the symbol of a dragon fighting a knight, and a virgin awaiting the victor. Then you stroll up the street, looking at the variations of that symbol on each letterbox, looking for your house. Trucks and army tanks filled with troops pass you by.

Everyone looks lazy. As you progress, the soldiers appear less and less formal. Some have no shirts on. Others wear only their Akubra hats. Pretty soon, you no longer see any uniforms. If you didn't know better, you'd think that civilians surrounded you.

There it is. As you enter your assigned house there are three soldiers lying around the veranda drinking beer.

"Where's the commanding officer?" you ask, and they point into the house.

Inside, a man is seated in the living room, watching television. A dragon is on the screen waltzing with a white-dressed virgin. The man doesn't look like a soldier.

"Sir?"

"Look," he says, annoyed at the interruption. "Just find yourself a room. Help yourself to the fridge."

"What on earth is going on here?"

He looks away from the screen and meets eyes with you. "Nothing's going on, mate. We're just waiting around for our orders to come in."

"How long you been waiting?"

"Not sure. Feels like years."

"But we're still soldiers aren't we? We're going to win this war, aren't we?"

"Eh? Oh, yeah I guess. Sure thing."

114

You get lost within the house as you try to find an empty room to put your bags in. Moving along the winding corridor you keep dropping bags and things and have to keep kneeling down to pick everything up. Every room you pass is filled with soldiers and Asian women, and one or two poker games.

Then you see one of your most cherished friends alone in a room. S/he sees you and smiles, and then asks if you want to help him/her on a trip out of the barracks – a mail-delivery mission.

Your friend takes you out the big double doors at the back of the room. You're outside now, and an Arabian desert stretches out before you. Bedouin warriors come and go on camels. You leave the outpost behind and follow your friend into the desert on foot. S/he doesn't seem to be carrying anything to deliver. You can't ask why not because you don't know the appropriate procedure for asking questions in a desert. Your friend walks ahead and begins to shed his/her clothes, piece by piece. The sun burns his/her flesh and smoke rises in a long ribbon that trails across the sky red and orange and violet and pink and metallic blue. The sky is grey underneath the smoke.

You see this as if you are not 'there' anymore but at the cinema, watching through the screen.

The person – who a second ago was your friend – is now a vaguely familiar woman. She walks naked and with good posture, not noticing at all that she is burning. The smoke is like a great banner across the sky. It climbs ever higher and longer.

Descending into view now is a small spacecraft, the size of a restaurant. It circles down and around the smoke and lands on the desert floor near the woman. The door opens and from it emerges a restaurant manager in a bow tie.

He shakes hands with the woman and says, "We saw the smoke; we got your message." He takes his jacket off and puts it on her, smothering the flames. Together they enter the spacecraft. From the waist up she is soot-black.

On the inside, the ship looks exactly like a restaurant – obviously a travelling one. It is filled with customers, all from the rich end of town, having a dinner party. The manager leads the woman to a propped-up chair for all to see, in a corner. She takes the jacket off and sits up there cross-legged. She is no longer blackened, as if the process was alchemical, changing her appearance like having had a face-lift.

The manager gives her a box of matches, which she uses to set fire to her nipples. This fills the room with pleasant incense. She lifts her arms, folds them behind her head and sits back against the chair. In the candlelight her skin looks like ivory and the nipples are erect.

In another corner, also propped up on a chair, is a man in wrestling tights. There's a textured roughness to his skin, and whenever he rubs his hands together coloured sparks fly, showering the customers. His penis is erect and when he rubs it a fountain of sparks flies from the end.

You are seated at a table now, eating with the other guests. A fat woman leans over to you and says, "Living sculptures, you know. I just love them!"

In the middle of the restaurant is a naked couple on a table. They are gymnasts of some sort. The man has slick-back hair and handlebar moustache. He stands firmly on his feet holding the woman up in the air. She stands with one foot on his erect penis (acting like a climbing peg) and the other on his shoulder.

The customers clap.

The woman bends forward and flips. She's upside down now, the pubic hair of her crotch sticking to the man's chest hair like Velcro. Her arms and legs are held out in the air.

The audience claps.

The man leans backwards until the woman's feet land on the table – causing the man to flip upside down. The woman now holds him up;

they've swapped positions.

The couple continue switching from manoeuvre to manoeuvre.

The people at your table are playing some kind of board game with the food. One man strategically moves a crab; a woman then pours some champagne on it. You try to follow the game but it's boring you.

You leave the table and dance. From a reflection in a window, you realise that you are both naked and female. As you dance, your breasts separate from your chest and swirl around you, like bubbles of liquid. The audience clap. It feels familiar. Someone calls out: "The latest in genetic engineering…"

All the customers are crowded around one table, arguing over the food. But as you move closer you see that instead of food, there are little model houses. The dinner party seems to have become more of a conference. The military guests discuss strategy over a scaled-down model of the suburbs.

Suddenly they turn to you and the other living sculptures. A military general yells at you: "GET INTO YOUR PARACHUTES, SOLDIERS! WE'RE ALMOST OVER THE DROP-OFF POINT!"

You and the other sculptures go to the showers

to clean up, but no water comes out of the taps. This is annoying because you feel greasy and dirty. There are paratrooper uniforms hanging on the wall. As you put a uniform on you realise that you have changed again to look the way you normally do.

"GO! GO! GO!" yells the general as you come out.

You try to ask him what your mission is but he pushes you out of the plane/restaurant without answering....

You feel a rush as you fall. The wind is whistling in your ears. When you pull the cord, time slows down and the parachute 'spills' out in a slow-motion puddle of white. The puddle spreads wider and wider as you float down to the street that you grew up in.

The white puddle is like a bog now that you wade around in. It's in the middle of the street and is sticky. Nearby, the man with the curly moustache is talking into a radio: "We seem to be bogged down in Suburbia..."

Finally climbing from the puddle, you find yourself right outside your childhood home. Soldiers are lying about on the veranda. You continue inside.

A loud explosion shakes everything. You crouch down. When you look up you see that the explosions are coming from the television – war movies, war footage, etc.

Over the noise, you ask where your old room is. The house seems to have changed since you grew up there. You see a dead relative and ask him about your orders.

"No such thing," he says. "I don't believe in a commanding officer."

Another explosion on the television shakes the house. Everybody hits the floor.

You need to get there – where the explosions are. That's where the war is. "How do I get there?" you yell.

Your dead relative yells back as another bomb explodes: "If you want to stay in the barracks you've got to pay the rent!"

"But the war…"

"Where are your priorities?"

Another bomb goes off. You leave the house.

There are television sets on every corner of the street. There is war footage on every screen. The explosions are very loud. Soldiers are running indoors for cover.

You go walking…

Eventually you realise that you are alone on the street and the explosions have stopped. On the television screens – some of which are as big as billboards – there are scenes of people shopping at malls or sitting in cafes. But you are completely alone in the street for as far as the eye can see.

And now, in the silence, you notice my voice for the first time.

I am talking to you and I have been all along. Keep walking up to that lookout point which overlooks the city. Sit down here on this bench and enjoy the view.

Now listen closely. As I talk, my voice gradually changes. It thickens and quietens. Eventually you feel you can see my voice in the form of symbols— words on a page. Yes, that's right. You are holding a book and I have been reduced to the words inside it and you are reading me.

Now look up from the book.

Your surroundings have changed, haven't they? Everything feels so tangible and familiar.

LOOK SMART SOLDIER!! THERE IS A WAR ON! Have you been awaiting your orders, going about in a dream like a jellyfish?

Fool! Nobody gives an untrained soldier any orders. First you need to train yourself. So put this book down and begin the training.

7.

The Black Newspaper

We are not waiting for death, though we know it is coming. Instead we think as little as possible about it. When we lay about on holiday, or on the weekend, staring out of our bedroom windows or moping about in pubs, surely we are waiting for strength of purpose. When this strength comes, I for one shall be able to tear my limbs free of this quicksand of melancholy and begin my work.

May strength come before death does.

I was waiting with a friend one night. We stood in his front yard watching time surge by overhead irretrievably, like two fishermen watching the fish swim by and with no line in the water.

Walking up to the front gate, Luca noticed that a long line of newspapers were scattered along the road. He called me over and we both inspected the pages. They continued in both directions so that we could not see either end of the trail of paper. The night sky was filled with bats, as usual.

Luca picked up one page and the headline said: "Flesh Eating Bugs Are Killing Our Children." Luca couldn't help but laugh at how fictitious it sounded.

I picked up one and read: "Waitresses Collapse Under Hollow Legs." All the pages we looked at were equally strange.

Looking for an end to the papers, I mused that they reminded me of J.L. Borges's Book of Sand, which had no definite end or beginning, like sand at a beach. So I suggested to Luca that we split up and each try to find an opposite end.

As I continued, I kept reading pages. One told of a man who had a succession of late nights and did not brush his teeth. The plaque built up so much that his top teeth stuck to his bottom teeth and his mouth sealed up. Another told of a stripper who spontaneously combusted whilst performing and rained ashes all over her audience.

Suddenly I looked up and noticed that the bats were flying overhead, parallel to the line of newspapers – a white path beneath me and a black path above. I picked up another paper and was surprised to discover that the words were printed as if in a mirror image. Looking up again, I saw what appeared to be white words printed on the black wings of the bats.

Without thinking, I reached up and grabbed one.

As I did I felt instant vertigo, as if the whole world flipped on its head. When I regained my balance everything was still again, but I was holding a black newspaper in my hands. Beneath my feet there was a whole scattered trail of black newspapers. Flying above my head was a long stream of white bats.

I looked at the paper and read the title, in white ink: "The Black Newspaper. Updates by the second."

By the second, I thought! That's impossible. What on earth do they cover?

Perusing the pages I was mystified to see an article about my ex-girlfriend who had moved cities. It didn't say what she was doing, but rather, the journalist had written, "I wonder what she is doing right now…"

Another article had pictures of various vans, all painted differently, but all with Wolfty And Cliff written on the side. The caption said: "Can't Wait For The Van, Thom Working On It Now…"

"This can't be," I said, rubbing my eyes. Wolfty And Cliff was the name of my publishing company, and they'd only published two books! Also, I was about to buy a van from a friend, once he fixed it up, so I could hit the road to sell my first novel.

I turned the page and saw the headline: "Strange Incident Involving Wolfty And Cliff Van: Discrepancy Over Black Newspaper Story."

I tossed the paper on the road with the others. Looking back, I could not see Luca, or an end to the black path. Looking ahead, I saw a man in a cheap suit clumsily picking up pages and cramming them into a leather briefcase. There were only one or two pages scattered behind him. It seems I'd reached the end of the path.

As the man came closer, I noticed that the road was painted up to look like the night sky. There were pictures of stars and clouds and even a moon.

"Good morning, sir," said the man. His skin was pitch black, and his hair was white and glaring. His irises were like two points of white light. It was intimidating.

"Morning," I replied.

"Damned wind," said the man. "I haven't sold a paper all night." He looked at me and squinted. "Say, you look like a man who wants to be informed. How would you like to subscribe to The Black Newspaper?"

"I already had a browse," I said. "To be honest,

I don't trust its integrity."

"You what?" said the man incredulously.

"I don't even understand your stories."

"The Black Newspaper is respected above all others, mate! Are you telling me you've never heard of it?"

"I don't think so. What exactly does it report on?"

"The world of thought. By the minute, too..." He held out a paper and I took it. "Whereas your local paper only covers the world of matter," he continued. "By the day, I believe."

"That's right," I said.

"Well, every event that goes down in the world of thought is captured right here. Not the events of the body: the events of the mind. You'd do well to read it – don't you want to know what you did yesterday?"

"I already know. I was there, after all."

"Rubbish!" he barked. "I dare you to try to rell everything you thought yesterday, in the order by which you thought it, and at what time you commenced each thought."

"Um ... well, no, I probably couldn't do that," I conceded.

"Well what about five minutes ago?"

"I remember thinking something about…"

"No – twenty seconds ago exactly. What was your thought?"

I hesitated. "I was probably talking to you twenty seconds ago."

"Probably, eh? My point exactly: you haven't the faintest idea what goes on inside that head of yours. All those lost daydreams! If you want to be informed about just what is going on in the world, there's no better publication than the one in your hands."

I looked at a random paragraph. Written there were the lyrics to the last song I'd listened to that night: "Oh Susanna, don't you cry for me: I've come from Alabama with a banjo on my knee..." It suddenly occurred to me that I'd been unconsciously humming it all the while.

"Just how many hours of each day are lost in darkness?" asked the man. "Find out here. Reasonable prices. An eye can't see itself, after all."

I thought for a moment then said: "I don't like this. It seems like you're feeding on the fact that I have poor concentration."

"Nonsense," he smiled. "We're helping you to concentrate. Showing you what you miss."

"What if I was to stop daydreaming and always keep my attention focused on a lofty ideal?"

"Well, we'd have very little news to cover. The Black Newspaper might even disappear. But that's not likely though, is it?" He pointed to another article. "Says here you're waiting for something."

"Yeah, purpose."

"Well?" He pointed to the newspaper.

I handed it back to him. "I'll have to think about it."

"Good, you just do that, mate. And we'll write about it…"

I turned and headed back.

After a while, Luca passed above me, riding upside down on a white bat. We both mirrored each other's shocked expression before the world started spinning again.

When we came to, we were lying on his driveway, watching the hordes upon hordes of bats that fill our night skies.

8.

The Duellist

Son – Are you afraid, Father?

Father – The duellist is never afraid. He is hungry. I crave victory, son. And so will you.

Son – They haven't arrived.

Father – They will – and you will learn much about English.

Son – But why? Can't you teach me through books?

Father – Don't be squeamish. Define a sentence, son.

Son – A sentence?

Father – Define it, boy.

Son – Let's see… an idea? One sentence is

one idea?

Father – No! For God's sake boy, you're thinking too passively, like an academic. Think like a duellist – what is a sentence?

Son – Sorry, Father. A sentence... it's, um, a ...

Father – Yes?

Son – ...a ... group of words, joined together to make a spear.

Father – Excellent son! A spear – with which to pierce the heart of your opponent. And a paragraph?

Son – A combination of attacks, I suppose.

Father – Yes, son. A flurry. You'll be a duellist yet.

Son – But why do we duel?

Father – Why do we speak? It's a pertinent question, son. From now on I want you to consider the motive for opening your mouth in any situation.

Son – It's communication.

Father – It could have been, but it's not. What happens when you speak, son?

Son – What do you mean?

Father – Are you giving or taking?

Son – I imagine it depends on the situation. And what you are saying.

Father – The situation – perhaps. The content – irrelevant. But let me put it this way: the crucial effect happens while you are speaking. Not before or after, but during. What does the other person do while you speak to them?

Son – They listen.

Father – Yes, son. They give you their attention. For as long as you speak, they give you their time. Do you understand the implications?

Son – We are but mortals, Father.

Father – Son?

Son – Time is limited. It is the most precious commodity. So they give us their lives!

Father – Excellent.

Son – Are we vampires, Father? Are we murderers?

Father – Don't speak that way. We are survivors. That is all.

Son – (Sighs.)

Father – What is the matter, boy?

Son – I shall never want to speak again.

Father – Don't talk rubbish. What I teach you is self-defence. What I teach is an art. Language is the gun and the subject matter is the ammunition. People fight and kill all their lives, albeit unconsciously; the duellist merely knows it. And the duellist knows how it works. He is skilful at it.

Son – Is everything so dark?

Father – Look around you, boy! Everybody

wants your attention – writers, film-makers, salesmen, preachers, politicians...

Son – My own father?

Father – (After a pause) Very perceptive, son. Yes: your own father. But what I take from you now will save your life later. I'm conditioning you. I don't need this attention from you; I have fame. My writings bring me all the blood I need.

Son – I'm sorry, Father. I didn't mean to say that.

Father – Be proud, not ashamed. You're showing quickness in thought.

Son – They come, Father. Over there.

Father – Then it begins. When they arrive, you stand by that tree and wait for me. But listen closely.

Son – Yes Father. What should I listen for?

Father – Identify what is what. Know which mutterings are attacks, counterattacks or parries. Follow the duel without being fooled by the subject matter – that is apt to change constantly. It is about me and him, nothing else.

Father – Morning, sir.

First Man – Good morning. Are you alone?

Father – I have my son, by that tree. But he's only here to learn.

First Man – Then shall we begin?

Father – Very well. Who'll start?

First Man – I will. It will only take me.

Father – We'll see. Choose your subject.

First Man – Music.

(The duel begins.)

Father – (Feeling his opponent out) Music? All right, but why -- what is it to you?

First Man – (Drawing the opponent in) I compose.

Father – Compose what?

First Man – Electronic music.

Father – (First attack) Then you have nothing to do with music.

First Man – (Dodging) And what do you mean by that?

Father – (Repeating the attack) You honestly call that music?

First Man – (Countering) You obviously don't understand the genre.

Father – (Parry) Perhaps not – but I understand music.

First Man – (Attack) Evidently you do not.

Father – (Counter) All right, what keys do you write in?

First Man – (A failed defence!) I don't know keys.

Father – (Etc…) What time signatures?

First Man – I suppose it is four-four.

Father – Suppose? You do not even know the language of music! How many hours do you practice on your instrument?

First Man – I told you, I compose. I have no instrument. Besides, there are many guitarists who don't understand keys. They only know chords and they rarely practice.

Father – They are not musicians either.

First Man – Then what are they?

Father – Imitation musicians. Beginners like you.

First Man – I'm no beginner. Music is sound. I arrange sound.

Father – Nevertheless you're a beginner. Language is arranged verbal noise. Should I toss out all the rules of grammar so that I can't decipher between an adjective and a verb?

First Man – No.

Father – There you are, then!

First Man – But what if I invent a new language?

Father – You do not even know the old ones, Beginner. Stop wasting my time.

First Man – (Angry/wounded) What do you know about it anyway! Bastard!

Father – I know keys and I know time signatures for a start. Stop wasting my time. Go and learn something before you mouth off!

Second Man – He falls!

Father – Who is next?

Second Man – I'll go!

Father – Very well, sir. Choose your subject!

Second Man -- Music seems popular.

Father – As you wish.

Second Man – I know music. I studied the piano seven years. I know the keys, the scales and the modes. I've played and learned with the best. Yet I respect electronic music. What do you say to that?

Father – So do I.

Second Man – You what?

Father – I also respect electronic music.

Second Man – But you just said you didn't.

Father – I did not say that.

Second Man – You implied it just then.

Father – You misunderstood. It was your friend's ignorance that I did not respect.

Second Man – …

Father – Well? Was that all you had?

Second Man – I find myself disarmed. You win.

Father – And you, sir. Step up if you will.

Third Man – Good morning. That was some brilliant fencing. Not necessarily right, but skilful all the same.

Father – One doesn't need to be in the right to win an argument. Choose your subject.

Third Man – I don't need any.

Father –You don't need a weapon?

Third Man – Let's not hide behind subjects. We both know what we're here for.

Father – Then I suppose the subject is fencing itself.

Third Man – If you like.

Father – You are an unorthodox duellist, I must say.

Third Man – I'm not a duellist.

Father – Then what are we doing right now?

Third Man – Talking. Conversing.

Father – Whom do you think you're fooling? What kind of trick is this?

Third Man – There's no trick. If you want my attention I'll willingly give it. I've read your works and I like them. You are a magnificent writer. Tell me about youself.

Father – You flatter your opponent?

Third Man – I'm not your opponent. I mean it: you're works are magnificent, even if your outlook is wrong.

Father – I already told you about right and wrong. As long as I'm winning, what does right and wrong matter?

Third Man – You're not winning.

Father – How's that? I've slain twice the number of opponents you have.

Third Man – You are an addict. You need my attention; I don't need yours.

Father – … I don't follow you.

Third Man – You are in a state of constant 'wanting'. I am not. Famous people get used to it and need increasingly bigger doses of attention. That's why you need to fight.

Father – Bah! Then why are you here if not to take from me?

Third Man – Only to share my view.

Father – To share! Ha! I don't believe it.

Third Man – Who cares what you believe.

Father – ….!

Third Man – I've hurt you.

Father – Nonsense!

Third Man – You're a brilliant duellist, no doubt. If I had taken a subject you'd have had me.

Father – You … you're wasting my time, fool.

Third Man – Then leave.

Father – … What?

Third Man – You are quite right, and I am wrong. So leave.

Father –….

Third Man – Am I stopping you? Keeping you here?

Father – Be quiet! Who do you think you are! Why won't you fight me, you filthy coward?

Third Man – It seems my friend that I have fought and won already.

Son – Father!

Third Man – He's fallen, boy.

Son – Why did you slay my father?

Third Man – I am innocent. You saw it yourself – I had no weapon with which to slay him.

Son – You … you had the truth.

Third Man – The truth does not kill. It frees.

Son – Then what did slay him?

Third Man – He couldn't use his weapon on me, so he turned it on himself rather than disarm.

Son – What kind of duellist are you?

Third Man – A new kind. We do not duel; we contribute. We share. We do not need the attention of strangers because we respect ourselves. We do not need to change others, for we are dedicated to changing ourselves.

Son – And where does one learn this way?

Third Man – It is largely self-taught. First you must strive toward harmlessness then the way reveals itself. Goodbye, boy.

Son – Wait! Whom do you fight for?

Third Man – I fight for all of us. And I fight

against that demon which is the urge to duel.

Goodbye, boy. Sorry about your father.

Son – (To himself) I'll learn this new fencing. And then I will kill the demon that destroyed my father!

9.

A Fighting Marriage

I used to work with a young woman who always looked busted up – like her boyfriend beat her or something. One day she lost the job on account of her broken hand. Can't work with that.

I asked her what happened but she never explained. "You're a hedonist," she said. "You wouldn't understand."

"How'd you get that broken nose?"

"That's my integrity. The raw wound, man, it shows you're a fighter."

But she lost the job, anyhow.

One day I was in an office and I saw my whole

life laid out before me. I felt depressed. I'd been getting in trouble lately because I'd been freezing up like how computers do sometimes. I stood up and stepped out of a line of desks. Gave some excuse to the boss but he didn't hear. Some 'upwardly mobile' young achiever jumped into my desk and took over – big opportunity.

That's when I noticed the girl was gone. The smoke from her cigar still lingered in the office, so I decided to follow the trail.

The ribbon of smoke led down the stairs and into the street. Standing around the footpath was a loose group of misfits including three tall men in business suits with identical peach coloured brief cases, their faces each painted up like mimes; a hustler with tan trousers and a beach shirt, his plumbing-pipe neck half a metre in height for the purpose of watching for police; a plump woman with ruby lips and zip-up breasts used as carry bags for pharmaceuticals; a muscular clown with gaol tattoos; a sitting dog taller than a standing man; a gypsy jazz guitarist with a twisted hand, busking with an upturned hat in front of him; a female escape artist dressed in a red one-piece bathing suit that glittered – manacles, chains and padlocks slung over her shoulder ready for the next gig; a pram, unattended.

The smoke from my workmate's cigar weaved in and out of these dalliers. I trailed it until I got to the pram. Looking inside, I saw a baby.

"Did you see a girl go by here? Smokes a big cigar. Cute-looking but with a cut under her eye," I asked facetiously.

The baby just looked up at me all stupid. Probably a member of some fraternity, waiting for a password, I thought.

So I kept on the trail of the cigar smoke. It led down some steps, into the train station, where I lost the trail.

I caught a train to the main street to get a tea and lament. To my surprise, when I got off the train the trail resumed; she must have caught the same train. It led, funnily enough, to a café on the main strip. It was a favourite café of university students. The trail ended at my workmate's cigar, almost finished, sitting inside an ashtray on an empty table.

I took her seat. Picking the cigar up, I took the last puff, blew a smoke-ring and thought, now what?

A waiter rocked up and said: "Can I get you something, sir?"

"Say," I asked, "do you remember the chick who sat here before me?"

"Big hair. Yeah."

"Can you tell me which way she went?"

"She's a student at the university. Probably went there."

"She's a student?" That was a surprise to me.

"Couldn't you tell by the cuts on her face?" shrugged the waiter.

The university was on the outer limits of town, on a hill. I did not feel good about approaching the place because it had a bad reputation. Word was that the university was very old, even archaic. They supposedly stuck to their own ways of doing things, ignoring the standards, practices and even modern discoveries of the rest of the world. The word was they still had a course in alchemy.

I walked up the path to the huge front doors. The building was like a rundown English castle. On the doors was a wrought iron cross with a rose entwined about it. The cross was an equal one – each of the four arms being the same length. I pushed open the doors and entered.

The students were very muscular, on account of all the heavy books they had to carry around with them. All these very big blokes strutting around, and me feeling intimidated. The women looked solid too, like ballet dancers.

"Are you looking to enrol?" asked a woman, noticing me.

"Um … is there a list of courses?"

"There aren't any courses, as such," she pouted. "This place is very specialised."

"Oh. What happened to your leg?" Her knee

was bandaged and she limped.

"A fight. Listen, go and see the professors over there." She pointed to a staff room.

Now the thing is I had no intention of enrolling. I was just looking for my friend. So I made like I was going to the staff room but kept on straight passed it and went up stairs.

I found myself in a library. I strolled past a whole section of books on grappling, jujitsu, wrestling, submission fighting, judo and the like. I stopped in the drunken kung fu section and opened a book.

"I heard you've been looking for me?" said someone behind me.

I turned around and there she was: 'Slick', the girl I'd worked with.

"How'd you know that?"

"A friend of mine phoned me," said Slick, "a little bloke in a pram. Why aren't you at work, Laird?" (Laird Kinthrop is my name.)

"Gave it the arse. Thought I'd see what you've got going. I'm very depressed and I've been missing you."

"Well, alright," she smiled. "You can help me carry some books then."

I held my arms out and she stacked the books on. Then the both of us waddled down stairs like a couple of donkeys, each with a stack of books.

On the way out of the building we passed an

outdoor class. The students were lined up in tracksuit pants. The professor went around to each student and punched his chest about ten times (in the case of female students, he only punched them in the stomach). That student would suck in some air and tense, in order to take the hits. After that, the student would beat the professor's chest. Then the professor moved on to the next student. And on and on.

"Check this out," said Slick.

When everyone had been beaten (the professor many times more than the others), the professor then beat the arms of the students. The students stood straight and tensed their biceps.

"What are they doing?" I asked Slick.

"Conditioning. So they can handle pain."

"But why?"

"They're students. The more you learn, the more you empathise with others...then sympathise. So you begin to feel their pain."

"Is that why the professor can take more?"

"That's right. Education is dangerous. A learned man will feel the combined pain of all cultures, everywhere. He starts to identify himself in everything he learns about. So if he doesn't toughen up, he could be killed."

"Damn!"

"Let's go."

Slick took me all the way to her home on the edge of town. By the time we arrived my legs were shaky and my arms were like lead. I just dropped the books and dumped myself on her couch. "Those books are so heavy," I moaned.

"Come on," she said. "Bring them to the backyard."

She went ahead, embarrassing me by how fit she was. When I finally picked the books up and dragged myself out the back, the girl was stacking some wood as if to make a fire.

"What's going on?" I moaned.

She ignored me until she had a small fire going. It seemed to me that there was not enough wood.

Just as I dumped the books down again, Slick told me to sit down on a rickety chair, facing the house. I did this with pleasure, and regained my breath.

She grabbed an electric torch and flashed it on the back of my head. It was so bright that it shined right through my head, making it transparent. It also projected the contents of my brain onto the wall. There it was, right in front of me: my mental map.

"Now you see this?" said Slick, walking around and pointing at the projection. She must have propped the torch up somehow.

"See what?" I replied.

146

"This is an inventory of your unconscious."

The projection looked pretty crowded.

"All this stuff here," she pointed at some numbers, "are your memories. This other stuff here is your fears."

"What's that big list of syntax?"

"That's all your prejudices."

"Shit."

"See these symbols? They are your desires."

"So much stuff crowded in there! Is that healthy?"

"No, man. I'm surprised you haven't been freezing up."

"Well, funny you should say that."

"You've got to clean out that psyche of yours, man. De-fragment."

She turned the torch off and I turned the chair around. The fire was almost out.

Without warning, Slick wiped her hand on my face, collecting a sample of my sweat.

"What's that for?" I yelled. The sudden contact took me by surprise.

"I'm just getting a sample of your will power," she said. "It's in your sweat." Then she wiped some of her own sweat and held her little hand over the fire. The sweat dripped down.

The second that the sweat hit the flames, the fire roared and doubled in size. It turned from a struggling little flame into a blue bonfire. I had to stand back it was so hot.

"Man, this is cool," she laughed. She started picking up the books and tossing them into the fire. "Help me."

"Are you kidding me!" I said. "They cost money, you idiot!"

But there was something about her you couldn't say no to. So I began tossing books into the fire. When we ran out, she went inside and pulled all the books from her own bookshelf. This took a while and it was almost midnight by the time we finished.

When the books were all under flame, we stood back and watched. To my surprise and her delight, the books did not burn; rather, they melted and fused together. Among her books on martial arts were also all the great philosophers of the East and West. The holy scriptures were there too, from all the major religions. Works of science were thrown in, from Darwin to Tesla and Einstein and on. The books all melted and fused together, until, eventually, there was only one book lying there in the ashes.

It was dawn. As the first rays of the sun blazed through, Slick fished the book out with some tongs. On the cover was the word 'Agni'.

"It means 'fire'," she explained. "In Sanskrit."

The book cooled while we broke for tea and breakfast.

We sat back, exhausted, and skipped through the pages. I could immediately see that anything outdated had been burned away. The rest was fused together in a new and hip way.

"Man!" I said. "This book is jumping!"

"Sharp as a tack!" she agreed.

"Let's get right down to studying it," I said. The book hadn't even stopped smoking.

"There's only one copy though," she said. "You're going to have to move in and marry me. Then we'll study it together and copy it out for wider availability."

"Okay."

At first, our marriage was as sharp as a tack. I'd awake each morning with the sun, and lick the bottoms of Slick's feet until she woke up. Then we'd get straight to the book. After reading it and discussing it, we'd plan what kind of stunt we would have to pull in order to apply what the book was teaching in our daily lives. This filled our days. By evening, Slick and I were completely pooped. But we were also happy.

After a few months, however, things began to go bad between us. The first thing was that Slick would go out without a word and come home with bruises and cuts. She never told me why, saying: "I don't see why you have a problem with it."

Can you believe that? People used to look at me like I was beating on my wife. Second problem was that I kept freezing up in the act of copying out the book. I'd just freeze for an hour or so and Slick would have to hit me with something.

Now, by this time we were running out of money. Nobody would give Slick any work because she was busted up all the time. And I couldn't hold a job because I kept freezing up all the time.

Slick didn't seem to mind about the lack of work, though, because it freed our days to work on the book. But, man, we weren't paying our bills.

So one morning after I woke Slick as usual, she said: "Forget the book today. If we don't do something about your health, you'll end up freezing permanently."

I yawned and said something negative.

"Come on," she said. "We have to save our marriage."

"Well … okay." She was right, after all.

She marched straight out the back and stacked some wood for a fire. It felt kind of romantic, like the first night when she told me to propose. Then Slick used some of my sweat to make a roaring blue fire.

"Okay," she said. "I want you to get as close to the fire as you can."

I stood right next to the fire. Straight away I

wanted to run – it was so damned hot! I stumbled back and said: "Why, Slick?"

"The heat will burn away all that crap you've got on your hard drive/brain. All the stuff you don't need."

Like she said, I could feel all the negative aspects of myself coming out in my sweat. Eventually I wasn't just sweating, but steaming too. My sweat wasn't clear liquid either – it thickened and fell to the ground in a tar-like puddle. It really stunk.

Slick had me near the fire everyday. As I became used to the heat, I was able to stand closer and closer. Finally, I stood right in the fire and let it burn.

When I stepped out, my body was tight and shiny like a sculpture that was once a big rock. I felt perfect!

Slick and I hugged.

"Now," I said. "We have to deal with these bruises of yours. Is it some girlfriend?"

"Nope," she smiled. "I once stood in the fire too."

"So what?"

"So look behind you."

I did so. The fire had burned itself out by now, and something was moving in the ashes. To my astonishment, I saw that it was all the sludge that I had sweated out. It was bubbling and growing and shaping itself.

Finally, it shaped itself into a humanoid and rose from the ashes. It was a bald and naked man, very similar in appearance to myself, though I had hair.

"You bastard!" it said. "You think you can get rid of me like some lame dog? I'm your personality. You're nothing without me!"

"Eh?" I said, surprised. "Beat it loser, before I slap you around like an example."

He walked up to me and handed out the biggest beating I'd ever had.

As I lay bleeding on the grass, he strode into the house and packed half my clothes. By the time Slick cleaned me up and made me a cup of tea, the 'bad me' had gone.

"Now you know why I always have bruises," said Slick hugging me. "I'm always meeting my own demon for fights."

"Shit."

The demon 'me' and the demon 'Slick' moved in together on the other side of town. While Slick and I worked on the book, the demons worked on something else. My demon had taken all the dregs and leftovers from the fire book and compiled it into another book. Whereas the fire book revealed unity and connectedness in all things, the other book focused solely on differences and separation. It was a compilation on everything outdated, on the forms of things rather than the quality of things, but to a quick glance it appeared to be a similar book to Agni. Therein lay the danger.

The other big problem was that, legally, the demon and I shared the same name and identity. So I constantly had to pay for his bills. He was a very expensive fellow, an utter consumer. He also loved drawing attention to himself and especially used his book to become well known. This affected me because I didn't want to be known for that atrocity. I felt I had to compete against the demon in order to keep my name honourable. In doing so, I was also stepping on his toes. Slick and I became regarded as a kind of modern day Count and Countess Cagliostro; half the town deemed us criminal charlatans and the other half deemed us saints. Sceptics sued me in court for things the demon did.

So my demon and I met every Sunday evening for a duel.

Slick and I were relieved when we heard that other people had begun making their own fires and burning down their books too. The One Book was being discovered everywhere within the old books. We weren't special. The load was off our backs.

Nevertheless, the fights went on.

But the fighting was a good thing, because

it kept us fit, sharp and always in training. If I gave up, the demon would use our identity for whatever it wanted.

But he always won the brawls, and I came home to Slick with new bruises each week, even more than her.

"He's too tough, Slick!" I whimpered one day.

"You need to enrol at the university," said Slick. "They've got all the knowledge on no-holds-barred fighting that you need. Plus, they have lecturers who will train you. Trust me. I'm about even with my demon now."

So I enrolled to learn how to fight, and waited for the semester to begin.

"The trick," said the man who was to be my professor, "is to keep on turning up. That's the hardest thing."

I was in his office, getting him to sign my enrolment form. He had the glasses of a scholar and the nose of a boxer, with scars over his eyes. "Every Sunday, year after year," he continued, chuffing on a pipe, "keep showing up to the fight, win or lose. And one day he'll fall." He pointed his pipe at me. "But don't look for it – just take his hits and come again next week."

There were still a few months before my first semester began. Rather than wait around, I did as advised and kept turning up to fight my shadow.

On my back in bed one night (awake due to an

aching rib), it dawned on me that that was what Slick had been doing all this time – keep turning up. The fights kept her fit, but they also kept her demon fit too. This led to much brooding.

The next time I met my demon, I did not fight. On sight, he struck me in the face. It brought blood. When I did not react, he tackled me.

Using an aikido manoeuvre, I freed myself, sending him to the floor. He got up huffing and dusting himself off.

"I've got that court case tomorrow," I said, as he squared up. "I'm answering for another of your debacles."

He swung and I ducked and circled.

"Shut up and fight," he snapped. "I don't care about your court case."

As he closed the gap, I said: "I'm pleading guilty."

This stopped him.

"Not just to that either," I continued.

His guard dropped to his waist. "Why?"

"I'll go to prison."

"Fool, if you admit to one thing, they'll prove another, and so on till your stuck in there."

"Exactly."

His mouth tightened and his eyes squinted.

"You look hot under the collar. Is there a problem?"

"No problem," he snapped defiantly. "What does it matter to me? I'll be free to continue."

"Until?"

He charged me, but I saw it coming. I simply ran the other way and kept running until he stopped chasing.

"Shall I spell it out?" I said, as we puffed together. "We share the same identity. If I'm in prison then you'll be neutralised. You can't do anything outside if it's known you're inside. And another thing, buddy: if I start taking credit for all your publications, you'll be redundant. You'll be broke."

He struck again, but this time I stood and took it. It had little power behind it anyway.

I said: "I'll take credit and responsibility for everything you did and nobody will notice you again."

He turned and walked the other way. I walked back to my hat, which had come off in the fight, and picked it back up. I turned to leave but he'd returned with a branch from a tree.

It broke on my skull and I was out for half an hour.

A few weeks later, I was still bed-ridden. My head was wrapped in bandages but I was recovering nicely. Slick nursed me through it, vexed that I'd been beaten so easily after all my study.

Then one morning she came in with a look of dread on her face: "He's here!" she whispered.

"Who?" I asked, sitting up in bed.

"You ... I mean your shadow. He wants to see you!"

"I've been expecting this," I sighed. "Let him in."

She did so, but stood in the corner with a cricket bat. Bless her.

'He' sauntered in bashfully, hat in hand.

"Well," I said. "How have you been? Bedridden, says the newspaper."

"Yes," he grumbled. "Apparently so. I see your point now. Nobody took me seriously, because the real Laird Kinthrop has been concussed. Nobody attended my lectures or bought my books. I simply couldn't have performed any lectures from a sickbed."

"The problem with sharing identities," I said. "You're a shadow. So do whatever you want: I'll take it."

"And if you're killed? Surely you won't go that far. It's a bluff."

"If I die, nobody will notice you again."

"Yes, you're right about that." He looked around as if for a chair, but remained standing. "But as long as you're behaving like this, nobody will notice me again anyway."

There was a short silence. He glanced at Slick

and then sighed.

"I find myself checkmated," he said. "That is if you aren't bluffing."

"So?"

"So what do you want? What are your terms? How can I continue, or shall you practically murder me in this quiet way?"

"You can have the past, man. Work with me and I can use you as a contrast."

"Work with you?"

Slick's body language was suddenly restless, or such was my interpretation.

"A before-and-after routine," I explained. "It's the only way to share an identity. What do you say?"

I extended my hand.

After a long pause in which a short cough was heard by Slick, he shook my hand. "I suppose I have no choice."

A week later we brought a solicitor in to make some kind of a contract. It involved Slick and her demon too. The solicitor explained that one doesn't make agreements with themselves: one makes what is called a 'vow' or an 'oath.'

"Do you swear it?" he asked us, after a long monologue detailing our arrangement.

"I swear it," I said, solemnly.

My shadow followed, and so did Slick and her shadow. Then we shook on it.

With regards to our work, we brought both books together to be looked at in relation to each other. Eventually they were published in one volume, with an 'old' and 'new' testament, so to speak.

10.

There Are Aeroplanes
In Our Auras

Down the street from the Irish pub, Steve Adams comes flopping clumsily along. He always leans a little too far back or forward, limbs swinging wide, eyelids only open enough to keep from bumping into things, and mouth wide and dropped, ready to sneer or smile depending on whom he bumps into.

He is only slightly drunk.

About him is a cloud of dark and light greys, with flecks of deep red peppered here and there. This auric cloud follows him along as if he is wearing it, although, the more we watch, the more we get the impression that 'it' is actually wearing or producing Steve (i.e. the colour changes and Steve reacts.)

As he rounds a corner the 'currents' of the dark aura flow to its edges and thicken there in certain places. These clots turn dark brown and then shape themselves into what look like bottles.

He reaches his house, walks in and dumps himself on the couch. The house is quite clean, just a little untidy. But his aura hasn't stopped working. The bottle shapes have hardened now into actual bottles with labels forming on them. Whenever a beer bottle is produced, it plops off the aura like a ripe fruit dropping from a tree.

When Steve's roommate Jay comes home, he finds Steve asleep, surrounded by empty beer bottles and stinking like booze.

A lit cigarette hangs from his mouth.

Jay, the roommate, has brought his friend Penelope home. Her surrounding thought-matter has the appearance of flailing hooks and waving tentacles. She moves around with a vague interest in not the present moment, but the moment just one more step into the future – the one just about to happen. But when it does, it becomes the present and she's already looking one step ahead again. She never sees what or who is directly in front of her. She is always in mid turn – her vision reaching around.

So, Steve was just a blur. Penelope noted him in her peripheral and said: "Hmmf. Steve's been out on the piss again. And who's going to clean up after him? You?"

Jay looks about and sees nothing unexpected. He then explains to Penelope that Steve does clean up, although it is usually days later when the mess has built up too much.

Penelope doesn't take this in, as she is not thinking about that anymore. Already she is looking forward to the kitchen where they will make coffee.

Penelope passes by to the kitchen. Although she is unaware, the 'limbs' of her aura swing down at the carpet and pick up a couple of beer bottles and cigarette butts on the way passed. Two of the tentacles are already clutching to a trashy pop magazine in one and a jacket in another. Her aura has collected a whole bunch of random objects, a visual record of her travels.

Back in Jay's room, Penelope is frustrated because of Jay's aura. She does not realise this, of course, but nevertheless his aura is holding her off, keeping them from bonding. As her aura tries to seep into his and become a mutual colour, his instead holds strong like oil in water, refusing to mix and refusing to take any of her random objects from her.

Eventually, Penelope says bye and leaves. Jay

notices that his room is messy now. Penelope's aura has left behind numerous cigarette butts, a beer bottle and a trashy magazine. She always does, Jay notes. Never deliberately, but he is always left with crap he does not want.

As he cleans up he notices, too, that her aura has unwittingly picked up some of his stuff and taken them – a CD and two of his most valued books. Unwittingly of course, so he cannot exactly get angry with her. Or Steve. He and Penelope are unaware of what is going on with their auras.

Jay goes to the television and turns on the news. The Prime Minister is giving a speech. His aura flashes the pale grey colour of fear. A little aeroplane is flying around inside it, now and then bumping into the Prime Minister's head.

Next, the scene cuts to another speech given by the President of the United States. His aura, much like Steve's, is producing fruit. Not beer bottles, though: little aeroplanes. The president's aura coagulates in blobs at its edges, the blobs shape into planes, then, when the aeroplanes are completed they fly away. To be specific, they fly into the auras of everybody in the audience within earshot. One even flies out of the television screen into Jay's aura, causing it to react with the pale grey colour. The president's aura continues pumping out planes like a factory from the industrial revolution.

The aeroplane in Jay's aura splits and reproduces itself. One of them flies over to Steve's aura and enters it. Steve tosses and moans in his sleep.

He is having a nightmare about planes flying into the twin towers.

10.

The Rooftop Yoga Sutras

Captain Friday awoke alone and sunburnt. He was lying on his back. When he sat up he saw that he had washed up on land and was stranded in the middle of Suburbia.

After climbing to his feet, Friday staggered to the nearest house and climbed onto the roof for a wider view of his surroundings. Maybe he'd see an end to the suburbs, he thought.

He did not, though. Miles and miles of identical little houses, shimmering under heat waves, lay about like rocks on a beach for as far as the eye could see. He might be stranded here for a long time, he considered. And he knew he'd have to start tearing down houses for material to make a shelter.

Upon entering his first house Friday discovered that natives inhabited it! The leader started yelling and making violent gestures, though he was obviously terrified of Friday. Friday could not understand the language so he turned and left.

So, this place is not deserted, he thought. Soon he discovered that, like sand crabs under rocks, natives inhabited nearly every house that Friday came across. Like sand crabs, the natives were also cowardly creatures. Try as he may, Friday could not figure out what it was they feared.

Friday climbed onto the rooftops and set up camp there. During the starry nights that followed, he pondered ways to find help. He felt immensely alone.

After a few days, Friday peered down into the house whose roof he was sleeping on. He discovered a lone native. Friday continued to study him, with anthropological interest, and soon discovered that the native had neither tribe nor family. He had been deserted at one point or another, it seemed, and Friday knew what that was like.

One day more natives came and threw the lone native into the street, yelling words like, "rent!"

and "job!" and "loser!"

Waiting for the right moment, Friday went down and helped the native to his feet. Grateful but confused, the native accepted the invitation to follow Friday onto the roof.

The native's name was Robinson. He was tall, lanky and gaunt. He carried himself with a tired hunch. Although the light blue of his eyes resembled a sunny day sky, they were sunken deep into his skull, as if retreating in shyness.

The new friends communicated with hand gestures, until, in time, they created a makeshift language between them. Friday told the brute that he needed food, and Robinson took him food gathering.

Friday cried in despair when he saw what the savages ate – they called it "takeaway food" or "TV dinners" – but he had no choice unless he wanted to starve.

Months passed by. Friday and Robinson stuck together, living like nomads on the rooftops. Friday tried to educate Robinson, teaching him all the things Suburbanites never thought about, and he slowly made progress. In turn, Robinson brought Friday the many things he requested: Suburbanite maps of the land, paper and pens, clothing and soap.

Friday immediately began a diary. He also

wasted no time in scrutinizing the maps to see where he was. But the maps were confusing – for example, he could not find the coast; the maps seemed to show endless streets of Suburbia, with the occasional change of terrain of industrial areas or ghettos.

"It seems to me," he wrote in his diary, "that my first task is to continue collecting maps until I find one with the coast on it. These maps, I must say, are rather primitive things and I am beginning to suspect that the natives here have never invented boats, let alone crossed the sea."

One morning, as Friday was going over his ever-increasing stack of maps, Robinson returned from food gathering. He was unusually wide-eyed and straight-backed. He babbled away at the top of his voice until Friday could calm him down. "Slowly," ordered Friday. "Slowly!"

Robinson managed to explain that he'd found another foreigner – a female – stranded in the suburban wilderness.

"By Jove!" cried Friday. "Where? Take me to her!"

After half an hour of roof hopping, Robinson led Friday down onto the road. He stopped at the front of a house as non-descript as any other – and pointed inside. Keeping a blade at the ready, Friday opened the door and entered.

The place was cluttered with oil paintings. Canvases were stacked against the walls and laid out on the floor. In the middle of it all was a pale woman, squinting into her latest painting with brush in hand. Her eyes were dark and commanding like Friday's. But apart from that, she could have been mistaken for any native.

She looked up at Friday.

"Ah!" she cried. Then she dropped everything and rushed across the room to Friday.

Despite having never met, Friday and the woman clung to each other and cried.

Over tea the woman, named Sunday, told of how she lived like a Suburbanite, and how she had even been accepted into a tribe. Friday asked if she knew which island they were stranded on and whether it was on the maps of the civilised world outside Suburbia.

"You're kidding me, right?" Sunday exclaimed.

"Why do you say that?"

Sunday squinted her eyes at Friday. "Do you even remember how you got here?"

"Not exactly," said Friday, standing up. Pacing the room, he said: "I was on my ship. There was a terrible storm. I must have blacked out … and I awoke here. I figure my ship was overturned, or I was hurled from it."

"I'm sorry, Friday," said Sunday solemnly, "but

I have news for you: this isn't an island. This is the bottom of the sea. You didn't wash up here on a wave; you sank!"

Friday tottered in disbelief.

When Robinson steadied him and helped him to sit back down, Sunday went on to explain that she was constantly trying to signal the surface. "I am sure there are search parties circling above," she added.

"But how would they know there's anyone down here?" asked Friday.

"I constantly send them messages in bottles. They float right up to the surface like air-bubbles."

"Prayers?" said Robinson, breaking his silence.

"Sometimes when I peer up towards the surface, I get a glimpse of something – I think it's a ship. I'm convinced they're trying to communicate." She gestured towards her paintings. "I paint the signals on my canvases."

"Oh," said Friday. "I figured they were just abstracts."

"We have to reach the surface," said Sunday.

Friday nodded in agreement.

From then on Friday looked to the sky. He could swear that on some nights he'd see a flash of light or a silhouette just beyond the blue. But, of course, it might have been his imagination.

Now that Friday was savvy to where he was, he also made a point to peer out over the Suburbs from his perch on the rooftops.

When he'd first arrived and seen everything slightly distorted, he'd assumed heatwaves caused it. Now he knew that all these bendy, wavy houses were actually under water. He'd thought that the heaviness he'd felt was from stress, and that the inability to focus stemmed from fatigue. What he took as humidity before, he now knew to be just plain sliminess. The natives are slimy people by nature, he thought, with their blank fish-like eyes and their purposeless wandering – like goldfish in a bowl. Robinson was no different, as fond as Friday was of him. Robinson carried that fishy stench with him everywhere like dreams gone old and rotten.

Whenever Friday looked up, he yearned to swim to the surface. Robinson assured him, however, that it was impossible. The Suburbanites believed that any swimming at all was impossible. Friday tried it but found he had no energy and couldn't make it. The horizontal currents were too strong.

Friday's Journal:
1. That which I have hitherto taken to be empty space (such as the sky) is, in fact, substantial.

They were in a house, studying one of Sunday's

paintings when she said: "You know, Friday, I suspect that there is a long history of sailors sinking to the bottom of the sea."

"Are you serious?" he replied. He was leaning into one of the pictures, a corncob pipe poking out from his teeth.

"Yes. From studying the tribe I live with, I think a lot of their culture and religious beliefs hint on the past presence of stranded sailors."

"If they died here," suggested Friday, "we should be able to find some evidence of them."

"Yes," Sunday agreed. "But if they managed to get back to the surface, then perhaps they also left clues as to how they did it."

Friday stood up and took the pipe out of his mouth. "Then we need to read up on suburban history."

"We'll get Robinson to guide us to a library. If there are any."

Instead of watching the sky, Friday began passing his gaze over the suburbs like a prison guard with a great spotlight. He noticed a peculiar thing: there were dark patches in the water. In fact, there were also cold patches and warm patches – just like in any waterhole. One night, Friday saw an angry young tribe roaming within a dark patch that had specs of crimson in it. It was not clear whether the patch was following them or vice versa. In the distance, he also saw a whole area tinged green like a floating ink spill.

"I need to spend some time down in the currents," Friday wrote, "if I really want to understand this phenomenon."

Friday's Journal:
2. This substance (space) is not uniform; it has changes and modifications.

The next morning, when the water seemed particularly clear and cool, Friday and Robinson set out to pick up Sunday and find a library. The current felt heavy. Friday felt as if he were walking in slow motion, pushing through the thick 'air'. They caught Sunday as she was leaving with her tribe.

"Where are they taking you?" Friday asked.

"It turns out that many natives are interested in my paintings," she said excitedly. "We're going to set up some sort of exhibition so they can view them."

"Remarkable!" called Friday, for they had not stopped. "Do you think they're interested in the world beyond the surface?"

"They can't be," Sunday said looking over her shoulder at him. "They don't even know of its existence. But the images are surely new to them."

"That must be it, then: the attraction of the new."

She stopped and turned around, as the tribe filed into a car. "Where are you going with Robinson?"

"To look for the historical records."

"Oh yes. Well, I'll catch up later and you can fill me in."

Then she climbed into the car and sped away.

They found a library. All the material was written in Suburban, but by this time Friday found Suburban easy to decipher; they had so many recurring words like "security," "work," "car," "house," "mortgage" and "football."

The "water" in the library was very cool and clear. Other Suburbanites were there too, reading.

Upon entering, the resulting waves of Friday's brisk movements went crashing into the other readers. They looked up at him, disapprovingly.

After a long search Friday could find no real evidence of foreigners in the books. He was not disheartened, however, because it suddenly occurred to him that he looked like a Suburbanite too, by now. The other sailors might just have easily blended in down here. The only clothes Friday could procure were Suburbanites' clothes: blue jeans, a pinstriped shirt, and black sneakers.

When he caught a reflection of himself in the window, he realised that the differences were only a matter of memory – his own.

I have no evidence of civilisation, he thought. If a Suburbanite were to ask me to give an example of one of our amazing inventions, I wouldn't have the faintest idea how to recreate one! I just used the inventions that others created. I'm a consumer like the Suburbanites.

On the other hand, there were Sunday's paintings. No Suburbanite can create anything like hers, Friday realised. She's not only painting the signals she sees, she copies images of our distant home from memory. Perhaps my diary entries will have the same uniqueness. Is this proof of the far-off land?

The one interesting piece of history that Friday found was the existence of unusual natives scattered throughout almost every era. The heads of these mysterious individuals were inside air bubbles! In other words, their heads were not in water – they were free inside these protective bubbles of air.

Amazing, thought Friday. Now, where else could these people get air from if not the surface?

Friday meant to discus his findings with Sunday, but he did not feel like leaving the rooftops. If he were to head to Sunday's camp/house, Friday would have to fight against the current, and it was moving pretty heavily in the other direction. Instead, Friday fell into a depression.

Day by day Robinson brought home new down-and-out natives. In turn, others would come uninvited. Soon enough they had themselves a whole tribe of rooftop gypsies – maybe twenty people.

After a month or so, Friday realised he ought to keep up his diary entries. As he took his diary up and looked about him, Friday realised that the patch of water his tribe were sitting in was of a brownish tinge. The clearness he was used to had gone.

It's the depression, he theorised. He entered it in his diary:

3. The space-substance is a principal in itself. While our thinking and actions affect its modifications, its modifications also affect us.

The faces of all the gypsies were long. All that Friday's companions ever did was hang their heads all day. Robinson had taken to drinking alcohol. Whenever he opened a bottle, the liquid would seep out and mix with the surrounding atmospheric liquid and affect the whole tribe. Ever so gradually, addicts of the brown colour would migrate from all over Suburbia towards the rooftops.

The cause of his depression, Friday believed, was the atmosphere. And in the excitement of this discovery, he ceased to feel down. The brown liquid backed away from him as if his excitement repelled it. He now sat in an isolated clear patch.

4. Emotions should be considered as weather. They are an external substance or force (part of the space-substance). Example: "I am not depressed – rather 'I' am being saturated by a substance called Depression."

Robinson viewed the change with a keen eye. Quick on the uptake, he decided to stand up and hop rooftops until he left the brown patch. To his dismay, however, as he broke away a cloud of brown did too, following him. He moved about in a brown bubble.

"It seems to be following you," called Friday.

Robinson looked wretched. He sat down and put his head in his hands.

Still feeling renewed, Friday – inside his clear patch – approached Robinson and pulled him up. As he did, the darkness of Robinson's bubble seeped into Friday's. The two friends hugged.

The brown colour mixed with the clearness of Friday's bubble until both men were inside a diluted bubble of 'Naples yellow.' This saddened Friday. He felt pity for his friend who'd had a hard life in the suburbs. Robinson, however, felt suddenly better. I'm not alone, he thought. Friday cares for my wellbeing.

"Come on," said Friday. "Let's keep moving. The brown of the others at camp far outnumbers our yellow. If we go back the liquid around us will darken for sure."

As they strode away across roof by roof, their bubbles gradually lightened and became clear again.

5. While the space-substance can be considered one large whole (i.e. the ocean), it can also be perceived as the accumulation of the little pools of space-substance surrounding each person and object. In this way we are all linked.

Friday and Robinson finally settled on a new roof to camp, away from the influence of the darker areas.

"We're finally making progress," sighed Friday, laying out his swag.

What they did not know was that their sudden departure had angered their former friends. The little tribe of rooftop vagrants began to gossip:

"They think they're better than us!"

"Went off on their own, did they?"

"Those two fools act like they have something to do. Losers!"

As the vagrants spoke, the sound of their venomous sentiments shot out jets of the brown colour. Speaking out loud was like sparking up gunpowder, or putting a match to petrol, only it wasn't fire that ignited, it was the brown liquid. Streams of brown liquid streaked across the sky in chain reaction towards Friday and Robinson.

Friday and Robinson did not consciously notice it, but they felt it hard! The negativity bombed them and darkened the air; the space surrounding our two heroes alchemised into the brown substance.

As the Depression began to stream up from Robinson and Friday in smoke ribbons – like the aftermath of an explosion – and the air slowly returned to its clearness, Friday and Robinson lay sprawled on their backs. Although unaware they'd just been attacked, the negative emotion reminded them of where they'd just come from.

"Those people were a waste of space!" blurted Robinson. "I'm sure glad I got away from them. I bet they're still doing the same old shit."

"Yup," agreed Friday. "They're pathetic."

This kind of talk perpetuated the brown liquid. It also started a subconscious 'gunfight'. The two camps fired off from their mouths, and the rooftops lit up a smoky brown and red. Soon there were two great dark patches, with a stream of darkness bridging the two. The rooftop war went on for weeks and both parties became used to it; in fact, they took it for granted.

"I saw what's 'is name – he's still doing the same shit." (POW!)

"Those bastards are so nosey!" (BLAM!)

Gossip became the background bombing from the two war trenches.

6. Through sound, we can use the substance to injure or to heal.

Friday and Robinson became fatigued veterans, continuing to fire out negative dialogue at the world in general. At this time they were addicted to the brown substance like junkies to hard drugs. To Friday there was no longer any war. He was merely an addict who followed his addiction. If ever the air became too light, Friday would blurt out dark comments or thoughts in order to produce the brownness and receive his fix.

It soon became apparent that the reason people climbed out of their lives and onto the rooftops in the first place was because the air/water was clear up there. Now that the rooftop gypsies were addicted to the murkier substances, the gypsies realised they might as well go back down to the streets.

So that is what Robinson did.

Friday, however, made a last attempt to kick the habit. He waded through the murky currents and headed to Sunday's house.

Her doors were open and removalists were running in and out, carrying her paintings to a big truck. She was there directing them. Friday noticed that the atmosphere was a bubblegum pink colour. His own brown bubble had trouble mixing with it, like oil and water. This made him feel uncomfortable.

"Friday!" called Sunday with a smile. "Where have you been?"

"I guess I kind of lost my way," he said bashfully. "But I'm back. I wanted to see if you've discovered anything about getting to the surface, through your paintings? I still believe we can make it…"

She looked at him blankly.

"Sunday?"

"Um … you know I still believe it too. But lately the Suburbanites have been paying top dollar for my paintings. So I haven't really had time to learn much from the pictures before I sell them."

Sunday began talking about galleries and tours and agents. Friday tuned out as she spoke. He noticed by her racy speech and dilated pupils that she was addicted to the pink substance.

Glamour, he thought.

7. If too much attention is given to the various modifications of the space-substance, they become addictive.

Friday snapped to attention, alone and sunburnt. He was lying on his back in a halfway house filled with other junkies. How long had he been there? He did not know, but judging by his long hair and Jesus-beard, it had to have been a year at least.

He was addicted to a whole variety of modifications now. He shivered with stress if he could not find the right patch of substance, and he migrated around the suburbs in order to follow whichever colour he needed at any given time. Various pastimes and employments were necessary to receive the relevant fixes they gave. Friday did not notice this consciously though because he'd neglected his diary. He thought he had free will. Everyone did.

Because of these intense addictions, and therefore the inability to relax, Friday's health began to fail. The murky modifications festered in and around him and soon he developed a grey, bumpy rash over his torso.

Friday went to a Suburbanite doctor, who performed all kinds of primitive tests on him. Finally, after weeks, the doctor called him back for the results.

The office, as is the tradition there, was painted white with white sheets and white curtains. The reason, supposed Friday, was to show how clean it all was. The space-substance, however, left over from many a patient and over-worked doctor was far-from-white. Downright murky, thought Friday.

The doctor was also dressed in the traditional white coat.

"Hmm," she began, her crow-footed eyes peering at him over the rims of her glasses. "There is no easy way to say this. I'm afraid that you're suffering from a terminal disease of which there is no known cure."

Friday broke down. "But ... how'd this happen?" he cried.

"The precise cause is unknown."

"Is it something to do with the modifications of the desire-substance?"

"The what?" The doctor appeared genuinely vexed. "I have no idea what you just said. All we know is that you are dying. Look, I'll show you."

She took out the skin-sample that she'd scraped from his torso, in order to study the rash. Now she put it under a type of digital microscope, the results of which appeared on the monitor of her computer.

Magnified, the rash looked like suburbia. The 'bumps' were shaped like houses, millions of minuscule houses, spreading over Friday and killing him.

Friday left, coughing all the way to Sunday's house.

Friday craved her these days. A small group (or 'clique') of Suburbanites moved around in the pinkish cloud. Friday, however, was addicted to Sunday's personal aura of pink. It had a hue of its own, slightly different to anyone else's, and Friday followed her to get regular fixes from her.

She didn't mind too much, because she made him pay with chores and favours and such. She was his dealer.

Inside of a stagnant pool of brown liquid bred all kinds of disease-ridden bugs. Robinson lived in a bad neighbourhood. You might say, instead, that this is where he lay dormant, like a corpse in a shipwreck. What he needed was an antagonist to the liquid, a trigger for change.

Whenever many streams of the brown modification crossed each other in one place, Suburbanites usually built a structure there. This was not conscious on their part, but the building marked such a place and served as a kind of 'heart-like organ.' Suburbanites called these, 'local pubs.'

This is where Robinson was.

The door flung open and his 'trigger for change' barged into the pub. When she entered the scene it was like adding one chemical to another chemical and causing the whole test-tube to change colour and start bubbling. The woman's particular hue was bright gold (a colour called Enthusiasm), which was a most powerful modification indeed.

Her name was Scoundrel. She was short, barefooted, and with huge dreadlocks. "Fuck!" she blurted. "How amazing is this neighbourhood! I just want to vomit with joy!"

"Hello," said Robinson, a bit dazed. "Where'd you come from?"

"Wow, look at you!" she laughed at him, approaching the bar. "You're a disaster! I love it!"

It was as if Robinson had just arrived, not her. The place had changed so much. As she spoke, he felt the heat from within her cause something inside him to spark up and generate heat too. He began to sweat, and his aura of brown began steaming and getting lighter.

Robinson bought her a beer, and it was the start of a beautiful friendship.

Being around her and her modification was

like taking medicine by prescription. He started rehabilitating, kicking his habit with regular doses of the gold colour.

At first, he was unable to enter her home. The space-substance there felt jolting and he tried to linger on the veranda as much as he could.

"Come in," Scoundrel would say. "This is Baroque!" as she put a side on her record player.

"I can't..." explained Robinson. But he could not articulate why. The atmosphere was too different and his junky cells reacted against this new environment.

As an excuse, he'd light a cigarette.

On one occasion she put on some pipe organ music. Robinson was able to enter this time but he still felt uncomfortable. There was something melancholy about it, which wasn't as hostile as usual to his general make-up.

"I have an idea," he said to Scoundrel. "May I borrow this record?"

"Of course."

Later, in his own flat, Robinson took out a black metal record. He realised that spiritual chants never sounded so beautiful as when placed in the middle of black metal songs. It was the contrast that did it.

Robinson played doom records, slow, heavy and dark music. He felt the music siphon out the brown substance. It externalised his Depression and thus served as an exorcism.

Afterwards, cleansed, he was ready for baroque.

This strange prescription of black doom metal followed by baroque and mystic chants enabled Robinson to finally dwell comfortable in the new environment of Scoundrel's home.

And all the while they generated heat.

During the weeks that followed, whenever Robinson travelled his golden aura acted as a buffer to the general currents of the suburbs. The streams of colour could not sway him, so they eventually went around him. This caused friction between modifications, and, in turn, the friction caused more heat. But it was a comfortable heat. Robinson felt warm. He felt he was changing. When a tidal wave of anger, glamour or fear swept a whole neighbourhood up, Robinson (on a successful day) remained unmovable (like Moses in the Red Sea).

On the unsuccessful days, Robinson at least observed the reason. He could tell when a wave swept by from the domino effect of people's speech. Gossip travelled in waves. Arguments and conflicts were obviously contagious; even those rushing in to stop conflicts got caught in them. Whole communities seemed to 're-say' to each other what their radios and 'local rags' said the night before.

The most effective defence for such waves of contagion was to hold the mouth closed. While the particular emotion still entered Robinson, his closed mouth stopped it from continuing on. Its momentum finished there, in him. And if it were too strong for him to hold onto, he would leave the scene and vent it. Black metal helped. Writing a diary helped. A boxing bag helped too.

Despite this renaissance of learning, Scoundrel did not stay long.

"There are too many adventures waiting," she explained then created a huge golden current and surfed away on it.

Robinson shed a tear. Despite all he'd accomplished, the very next moment he was drowning in Depression.

With grinding effort, he pulled himself together once again, and went to find Friday. He searched all the brown patches and fashionable pink patches but Friday was missing in action. "Where is that dude?"

Then, in the distance, Robinson spied a single house covered in a patch of liquid that was almost black. With a fearful shudder, Robinson headed over to check it out. Robinson circled the house, keeping on the edge of the blackness. "Friday!" he called "Are you in there?"

No answer.

"Is anybody in there?"

A moan from within.

I'm just going to have to make the sacrifice, Robinson thought.

As he entered the black patch his golden aura mixed with the darkness, unable to hold out. The whole scene reached a balance of a very dark grey-brown, and Robinson felt depressed as Hell.

He shuddered and went weak at the knees.

Friday was inside – his head on a table, cigarette in one hand, glass of booze in the other, beard and sweat-stained clothes.

"Friday…"

"Hello Robinson. You don't know how much better I feel seeing you again."

"You look like shit."

"I'm dying. There is nothing to be done."

"Says who?"

"A doctor."

"A Suburbanite doctor, no doubt."

"So what?"

"So – you're a sailor! You need someone who understands the sea."

Robinson tore the alcohol away from Friday and shook some sense into him. "Come on, you fool! It's this black cloud that's killing you. To the rooftops!"

The first thing that Robinson discovered – or rediscovered – once they relocated back to the rooftops, was that moving to another location does not get rid of your problems. The dark cloud followed them. Robinson would have to figure out a way to shake it off.

He tried death metal and black metal, but this was ineffective. He tried classical music. There was a slight improvement in colour. But only slight.

The problem was that the 'almost-blackness' (shall we call it coffee?) could not disperse because of a surrounding membrane, holding it in. Neither Robinson nor Friday felt motivated. They were, after all, stuck inside a dark cloud. So, as Friday gradually withered away, Robinson considered taking up an addiction. He was not sure which one yet.

In his boredom, Robinson thought of Scoundrel. By association this led to thoughts of how he'd stopped the chain-reactions when he was with her. He must have helped many people inadvertently, he thought.

With this thought, the membrane burst. The 'coffee' began dispersing. Simultaneously, a spark of Enthusiasm was created, and that streamed out too.

Robinson's boredom remained. He went through

all their belongings and began to browse through Friday's old diary. He read all the existing entries and realised that he had acquired new information. So he entered it in the diary. He felt the heat from within again.

(For consistency's sake, Robinson imitated Friday's style of writing.)

8. The modifications and currents of the space-substance can also be used to aid you and propel you, providing you are not addicted.

9. The way to resist addiction is to see the substance as it is (Not Self), and to focus solely on its opposite (Self).

10. For those already addicted, Enthusiasm is a cure. (Not to be confused with Passion.)

11. Self-absorption creates a membrane around you. This creates a 'stagnant pool.' Awareness/consideration of others bursts the membrane.

12. Most speech is involuntary, caused by domino effects of one or other of the modifications. The first step to free will is to resist speaking.

13. As the space-substance is made from emotional-mental matter, our speech is the indication of what quality of matter surrounds us.

Robinson began, once again, to feel the golden substance stream his way. He aided this with various music records and books. He sat every morning with closed eyes so that he could focus all of his attention on the fire within him, forgetting the sea. The fire burned ever brighter, and his aura slowly dissipated the dark cloud.

By degrees, Friday began to recover.

Robinson added more to the diary and encouraged Friday to take up recording again. Obediently, Friday reread the whole diary. The last entry was:

14. Certain habits make and keep the space-substance still and clear. This allows the sun above the surface to be seen.

When Friday read this he almost did a backflip. "You mean to say," he cried, "that you have seen the sun?" He clung to Robinson in admiration.

The truth was that Robinson only saw glimpses of it – a golden light, twinkling either far above or within himself. But Robinson's new entries were enough to shake the darkness from Friday.

When he took his shirt off, Friday discovered the rash had disappeared.

From then on, Friday's days were spent studying the last few sutras and doing experiments with speech. He took trips down to the streets to transform the information from theoretical knowledge into practical wisdom.

As his outer aura cleared, he spent time viewing it and saw that it still had traces of all the addictions he once had. The heat he felt from the aura of the diary (for it had one) and Robinson, however, made Friday sweat these impurities out.

Friday added this:

15. When one is subject to outer heat, this is the beginning of the road to purification. The outer heat can take many forms (i.e. people or books, etc.). It causes one to sweat away the impurities in one's own personal pool of space-substance.

16. The outer heat then sparks up the Self, the fire within. This causes friction with the outer world, the sea, and produces even more heat.

"You seem back to your old determined self," smiled Robinson one day.

Friday, who was sitting straight-backed and eyes closed, merely smiled in response. He was concentrating on clearness.

17. When the currents of the seabed, and the seabed itself, cease to hold any interest or appeal for you, this means you are ready to begin the journey to the surface.

Robinson took care of all daily tasks like finding food, cooking and making camp. Friday spent an increasing amount of time concentrating his mind on the surface. With eyes closed he sat all day long as still as a house. Robinson saw that Friday's aura was clearer than ever, and Robinson realised that what they'd previously considered to be 'clear' was only comparatively clear. In comparison with Friday's aura, Robinson's was still a little murky.

One morning, upon waking, Robinson looked over at Friday and saw that he was already awake and in meditation. To Robinson's awe, he saw that a pillar of clear water extended from Friday up towards the surface. A stream of down-pouring light shone from the surface and illuminated Friday. It seemed to Robinson that Friday now had a little sun inside his head (perhaps a reflection of the real sun above). Its ray lit up the rooftops like a lighthouse. Then the sea began to boil around Friday.

Friday appeared translucent, almost as if his body was itself a modification of space-substance/

water. The shaft from Friday's head to the surface began to twist in movement, becoming a whirlpool.

Robinson sensed that his friend would not be around very long. Sure enough, an air bubble zoomed down from the surface and stopped when Friday's head was inside it.

Friday opened his eyes, an expression of absolute peace on his face. "Robinson, pass me the diary," he said.

Robinson did so and Friday made his last entries in it.

For the next few days, Friday sent golden currents down into the suburbs, trying to clear the water. The different modifications dissolved little by little and became clearer. But as the suburbs were so vast, Friday could not clear it all single-handed.

Finally, Robinson saw that Friday's 'sun' burned so intensely that Friday's aura steamed and scattered. There was now no personal pool at all between him and the surface. Next, Friday's actual body began to bend and bubble. Friday smiled at Robinson, as Friday turned completely transparent. Then his body broke apart, setting the sun free.

As the body of Friday scattered and joined the general space-substance, the 'sun' that was inside him expanded and formed a new golden body of light. As if by the power of a vacuum, he shot straight up to the surface ... and out of Robinson's sight. The water around Friday parted in a pillar of fresh air.

Within the hour, the water returned to normal (only cleaner).

Robinson cried. All that was left was Friday's teachings on how to follow.

The soul that had been Friday burst through the surface of the water. When he did, he breathed in – for the first time in who knows how long? – pure air. The world above seemed so bright, with no thickness and no currents at all.

The soul formally known as Friday cried out in relief. All around him were sailing boats and rafts of varying sizes. On the boats and flying around in the air nearby were angelic-looking sailors. They were glorious in navy whites and sailor hats tilted over their foreheads. A bearded sailor extended his hand and helped 'Friday' up, onto a raft.

"Welcome back, matey," said the man. "Mission accomplished!"

As soon as the sailor spoke, Friday's memory flooded back. His boat had not overturned. He hadn't been hurled from his ship. He had deliberately dived down into the sea in order to help retrieve the other sailors who'd become stranded on the bottom of the sea. Friday had been responding to a message in a bottle!

To welcome him back, all the other sailors sang – in choir – a traditional sailor's song of welcome. Many of them broke into tap dance.

Through years of excessive addiction to all the various modifications of the space-substance, Sunday had become immune to it all. She had needed stronger and stronger doses, until nothing hit the spot for her at all. Suburbia, as far as she was concerned, had nothing to offer her anymore.

So, in desperation, she went wandering. After much aimless wandering, she began to contemplate suicide. But just as she thought this, she stumbled into a strong current.

It swept her along and seemed to give her aura an enema. In the distance, the stream led to the rooftops but was anchored down in the suburbs by a book. It was as if the book, which she saw in an acquaintance's hands, was a sinker on the end of a fishing line.

"Be quiet," she said to her acquaintance. "What is this book you are babbling about?"

Her exited acquaintance (a fellow painter) handed over the book. It was called, The Rooftop Yoga Sutras of Captain Friday. Edited by First Mate Robinson.

"I've met these people," explained Sunday. "I'm sure of it."

In a week or so, Sunday went to meet this so-called 'patron Saint of the Suburbs.' Though Friday had passed on, Robinson sat on the rooftops in prayer and contemplation. Disciples sat around him.

Just entering into his presence filled Sunday with a feeling of relief, as if a heavy burden had been dissolved.

"Take me as your disciple!" she cried.

"My disciple?" he smiled. "You are a sailor! I'll tell you what. Come and live with me on the rooftops, and together we will help each other to follow the sutras."

She cried some more, this time with joy.

A routine developed, wherein Robinson often played water-clearing music and did water-cleansing exercises. Sunday joined in. They both reproduced the Rooftop Sutras in order to give them to others.

More people came. Hordes gathered around to hear Robinson's lectures. Robinson, well aware of his imperfections, spent the evenings studying Friday's last entries.

18. When the sunlight streams down unhindered, all that is liquid heats up, bubbles and dissolves – revealing the sailor as he truly

is.

19. The Self/sailor, free from his sea-body, is now weightless. He floats up to the surface and to paradise.

Robinson added one last entry:
20. Once free of the ocean, the sailor may choose instead to remain under water in order to help his brothers and sisters arise too.

In time, more Suburbanites became fed up with being tossed about on the currents. Family by family, town by town, they climbed onto the rooftops. It was a show of unity. They were finally united in their dissatisfaction with the old lifestyle.

It was a mass exodus of Suburbia.

11.

The Witness

For a long time I wasn't sleeping well. I'd stay up all night and I'd go to the waterfront all by myself and watch the sea. That's when I discovered the secret of performing miracles. I was sitting there on the wharf with my feet dangling over the water. While lost in thought, I jumped down and began pacing.

After a moment I realised I was walking on water.

I looked around feeling very guilty. After all, I was doing something I wasn't supposed to be doing! When I was sure nobody could see me,

I came to the conclusion that one can perform miracles just so long as nobody is watching.

Go ahead – try it.

Well, we'll get into that later. Where was I?

Full of enthusiasm, I kept walking across the water until I lost sight of land.

Eventually a boat appeared over the horizon. It was only a lifeboat. As it came closer I saw that three monsters of differing sorts populated it. Now, I'm well aware of the fact that a lion would be called a monster if we weren't familiar with its species – so familiar, in fact, that we named it the lion! But I did not know what these beasts were called, so they were monsters to me. They all had large sabre teeth. One had a horse's head and a woman's body; the middle one was tall, thin and grey-skinned, with an old man's face and pitch-black eyes; the last monster was a huge bird-like animal but with a beautiful woman's face.

Because I was no longer alone, I lost my ability to perform miracles and fell under the waves.

Lucky for me, the three monsters lifted me into the boat as they passed by.

"Thanks," I said, soaking wet and pressed in the middle of my saviours.

"In all honesty," said the horse-head, "you shouldn't thank us. The truth is, you see, we only saved you so that we could rip you to shreds."

"Oh I wouldn't do that if I were you," I said,

thinking quickly.

"And why not?"

"I'm a human."

"Rubbish."

"It's true – look at me."

The old man-monster looked at me keenly. "I doubt very much," he said, "that a human could be found out here all alone with no boat."

"But here I am. What other creature am I?"

"An ape."

"So you find it difficult to believe a human would be out here, but you'd believe in the possibility of an ape?"

"He has a point, Moirtex," said the horse-head monster to the old-man monster. "Besides, apes have much more fur."

"I say," said the bird-like animal with the beautiful woman's head. "I fail to understand the significance of his being a human. So what if he is? We can just as easily rip a human to shreds as any other creature."

"Oh dear!" exclaimed the horse-head. "You can't go killing humans. A least not when there's only one."

"That's right," joined the old-man monster named Moirtex. "If he had a couple of friends with him we could kill two of them."

"I'm afraid I don't understand," said the monster with the beautiful woman's head.

"We humans," I explained, "are the eyes of the universe."

"The what?"

"We are the only species who writes things down, who record history. We are the witnesses of creation. A thing doesn't exist unless it is witnessed by us ... imagined or theorised, at least."

"I'm not following..."

"If you were to do away with me, you would cease to exist."

"Is that true?" the woman's head asked the other two monsters.

Moirtex said: "Yes, he's quite right, Louzvoo. It's the duality of the universe. For a thing to be known, you need a knower. For a thing to be perceived, there must be a perceiver. They're like two ends of the same stick."

"We only just met him, though," noted Louzvoo. "Did we exist before we met him?"

"I doubt it," said Moirtex.

"That would be impossible," said the horse-head.

"Well, he's lucky I have a short memory," said Louzvoo.

"You are just as lucky, my reluctant friend," I said to the woman-headed bird.

"Oh yes? And what about knowledge itself?"

"What do you mean?"

"Well you have the knower and that which is known – but what about knowledge itself? Knowledge as a factor or concept: the act of knowing."

"I think you've just brought the universe from a dual nature into a triple nature," said the horse-head.

"But how does that change things?" I asked.

"It connects the two, perhaps?" said the horse-head.

"But does it save this man?" said Louzvoo. "If he ceases to exist, there will still be humans around somewhere who acknowledge that there are more things to know than what they already do: we might come under that category. Acknowledging our possibility might keep us existing."

"That's sounds like a risk," said Moirtex. "To kill him or not to kill him?"

"Why don't we sleep on it?" I suggested. "That way we can let the wisdom that comes through in dreams instruct us."

About an hour later everybody was snoring except for me. As they slept I stepped out of the boat and jogged quietly away. I secretly knew that if they had killed me, they would have continued to exist, but I was glad the bluff worked. If I had died, there still would have been one human witness: you, the reader.

Then again, if I had died, I would not have written this down. But on the other hand again, I might have survived to write in my own death just to make the story more action packed. It was a risk.

It was morning when I reached the waterfront again. I was very exhausted and the sun was up. I went home and straight to bed. I've never had trouble sleeping since.

The one thing I did not understand was this: how on earth was I able to perform miracles when I wasn't ever alone; you, the reader, were present and observing me all along!

My only conjecture is that you, the reader, must believe in miracles (at least when framed in art or jotted on pages, like the conditions for a magical rite). That way, I wasn't going against any majority belief system.

When you think about it, Christ was rarely alone when He performed miracles, and His audience actually asked Him to help on most occasions. (When He was in His hometown, it is said He had great trouble in healing the sick because of the lack of belief in the citizens.) But even when He was away from any human eyes – there was always that one alleged witness ever present: His Father.

To the writer, then, you -- the unseen collective of potential readers -- are God; for

what is a published piece if not an act of faith
that someone is listening?

12.

The Divine Jigsaw Puzzle

Biologists say that every cell in the body rejuvenates itself thirty to fifty times in a life. After that the cells can no longer split and copy, and the body dies. So, with new cells regularly replacing old ones, every few years we each have an entirely new body. These building blocks could be likened to jigsaw pieces collectively making up the one picture.

In the middle of the jigsaw puzzle (within the head) there is one odd piece. This piece belongs to a different picture than the others. While the rest of the pieces are replacing themselves, the odd piece inside the head remains unmoved and unchanged during all fifty rejuvenations. This tiny piece is the point of consciousness, or the sense of 'self'. It longs for the rest of the picture that it is compatible with. At death, when the other pieces have withered away, this odd piece still remains unchanged, though also unseen because of its minuscule size. It then restarts the process of attracting around it a whole new puzzle of jigsaw pieces. Its hope, try after try, is to attract more and more pieces that are from the same puzzle as itself, therefore making it no longer an odd piece. This is reincarnation.

Certain experiences cause change within the entity. They spark up the 'odd' piece so that its attractive force (its 'longing') becomes slightly more powerful. This may cause one of the other jigsaw pieces to replace itself with a new 'odd' piece instead of copying itself as usual. If the experience inspires the entity to go further and experiment with his/her lifestyle, the new experiences will cause the changing of more jigsaw pieces for odd ones. Now that there is a group of odd pieces a second picture appears. This is evolution, or the consciousness expanding.

Well-trodden experiences that are inconsequential cause no change. The point of consciousness then remains outnumbered by the surrounding temporary pieces. It also remains powerless against their impulses. All the material urges, the biological and emotional addictions, are forces that hold sway on the temporary pieces. One addiction sends the person one way, a hedonistic urge draws him/her the other direction. And so on. The conscious spark or odd piece is outnumbered and powerless to take control. This is cause and effect or karma.

The active seeker, then, seeks out the experiences that will provide him/her that first spark towards taking control. In that sense we are what we surround ourselves with. Ever so gradually, after the battle for supremacy between the lower and higher jigsaw puzzles (it is as if the body is a board game), the person becomes transformed cell by cell by pieces akin to the unit of consciousness. This is transfiguration.

The Undergrowth collective is an evolving organism of writers, artists, media makers and cutting edge onto-logical guerillas.

Undergrowth publishes an online and print magazine containing short fiction, journalism, poetry, visual art, photography, comics and esoterica from Australia's counter-cultural underground.

Our website Undergrowth.org hosts an e-book library of emerging and established authors in downloadable PDF form, on-line art galleries of contributing artists, music videos, spoken word and audio interviews available as podcasts, video documentary clips, short films and animations, community forums, music and the ongoing Nomadology travelling blog project.

We are all change agents.
Engage the flow and swim with it.
In it.
Become it...

{we live not Underground, but in the Undergrowth}

Recent publications from
Undergrowth Inc.

Nomadology: Navigating A Globalised World

Crossing from the personal to the political, local to the global, NOM-
ADOLOGY is an anthology of blogs, anecdotes, gonzo
journalism, poetry and reflections by digital gypsies on the
nature of travel in a globalised world.
http://www.dislocated.org/nomadology

The Journeybook: Travels on the Frontiers of Consciousness is an
anthology of art & writing on altered states, contemporary psyche-
delic culture and the history of shamanism. Including writing from Rak
Razam, Dennis McKenna, Erik Davis, Tim Parish, Daniel Pinchbeck & Ter-
ence McKenna.
Read on. Tune In. Discover.
http://www.thejourneybook.com

Mercury by Si

Si is a poet & performer based in Melbourne. Mercury is his first book of
verse. It includes the Victorian Poetry Slam Championship winner 'This
City Speaks to Me.'
http://undergrowth.org/mercury

ALUC(i)NA by Benjamin J. Wild - The first anthology of poetics by vaga-
bond wordsmith Benjamin J. Wild.
http://undergrowth.org/alucina

Portals by Timothy Parish

'Portals' is the first anthology of writing by Timothy Parish, co-editor
and art director of Undergrowth.org. A personal journey through geo-
graphic/political and metaphysical landscapes collecting short stories,
poetry and journalism from over five years of travels.
http://www.undergrowth.org/portals

For more information or to purchase these titles go to:

WWW.UNDERGROWTH.ORG